KILLER'S CORRAL

Center Point
Large Print

Also by Merle Constiner and available from Center Point Large Print:

Death Waits at Dakins Station

This Large Print Book carries the Seal of Approval of N.A.V.H.

KILLER'S
CORRAL

Merle Constiner

CENTER POINT LARGE PRINT
THORNDIKE, MAINE

0280164

This Center Point Large Print edition
is published in the year 2019 by arrangement with
Golden West Literary Agency.

First US edition: Ace Books

The text of this Large Print edition is unabridged.
In other aspects, this book may vary
from the original edition.
Printed in the United States of America
on permanent paper.
Set in 16-point Times New Roman type.

ISBN: 978-1-64358-135-4 (hardcover)
ISBN: 978-1-64358-139-2 (paperback)

Library of Congress Cataloging-in-Publication Data

Names: Constiner, Merle, author.
Title: Killer's corral / Merle Constiner.
Description: Large Print edition. | Thorndike, Maine :
    Center Point Large Print, 2019.
Identifiers: LCCN 2018059091| ISBN 9781643581354
    (hardcover : alk. paper) | ISBN 9781643581392 (pbk. : alk. paper)
Subjects: LCSH: Large type books. | Murder—Investigation—Fiction. |
    GSAFD: Western stories.
Classification: LCC PS3603.O559 K55 2019 | DDC 813/.6—dc23
LC record available at https://lccn.loc.gov/2018059091

KILLER'S CORRAL

I

JOEY WAS SITTING at the kitchen table with his father, unwashed breakfast dishes in the sunlight between them, when his father, a grave, grizzled man with a bulldog jaw, said quietly, "Leave the room. Now. Go upstairs somewheres, and hide in a closet. Whatever this is, it might be trouble."

Through the window at his elbow, the nine year old saw a man walking in the garden, toward the house. You didn't have to look twice to see he was the meanest kind of riffraff. His bloated face was unshaved and depraved. His denim pants were out at the knees, showing grimy skin as he stepped. He wore a sleazy red and white candy-stripe calico shirt, and the nickel gun in his holster, while a giant, was cheap and tinny looking.

There was a man at the garden gate in chaps, mounted, just waiting, and on the hillside which blocked the rear of the house a third dismounted and sat on a boulder, with a rifle at the ready in the crook of his arm. All three were strangers. "Scoot!" ordered his father. "This ain't no way for folks to come visitin'." His gunbelt was upstairs on the bedpost, but he didn't seem overly alarmed. Somehow, he never seemed alarmed.

Joey moved, but not for the hall. Against

7

his father's frown, he dashed for the corner cupboard. This cupboard, built under his mother's specifications just before she had died, had been one of her favorite pieces of furniture. It was constructed of oak-stained poplar with two doors faced with ornamentally perforated tin. Inside, there were shelves above, a large compartment below.

Joey got hunched into this compartment, and got the door shut, before the man in the calico shirt entered.

Entered without knocking, his big nickel pistol in his hand.

Enjoying himself, he said, "Just hold it, friend," and gave a shrill vibrating whistle.

Joey could see him plainly, but in a mottled sort of way, through the perforations in the metal. He was so close where he stood that Joey could even smell him, his stink of filth plus what must have been an asafetida bag inside his shirt to ward off illness. Almost immediately, he was joined by his two companions from outside. Close up, they looked as depraved and scummy as their friend. Their guns, too, were drawn. One of them was an elderly man, all bones and tight skin, and the other, the most intelligent looking of the three, was mainly noticeable for the red silk neckerchief he wore, and for his gunbelt. His gunbelt was broad, expensive looking, of carved leather, with the picture of an eagle with a snake in its mouth. The emblem of Mexico. Mexican craftsmanship.

It was this man who did the talking.

He asked, "You Rann Clark?"

"Yes," said Joey's father. "And who are you?"

"President of the Clark Road Company?"

"Some call me that."

"Under government contract?"

"Right."

"They tell me," said the man in the carved leather belt, "that the government is mighty free and easy with its spending when it hands out its contracts. You must be a rich man."

"The government doesn't just hand out its contracts," said Mr. Clark. "You've got to bid on them like any man. And they've got financial experts to keep you reined in decent."

"You got a nine year old boy," said the man. "Where is he?"

"Away," said Joey's father. "And where is any boy when he's away?"

"Where's your strongbox?" asked the man.

"I don't have a strongbox," said Joey's father. "I don't need one. I'm not paymaster."

"Who is paymaster?" asked the man.

"The government," said Mr. Clark. "A lieutenant up at the fort."

This was a blazing lie, Joey knew. Rush Ledderman was the paymaster, just as he was actually the company itself.

"Where are your stables?" asked the man. "I didn't see 'em as we come in. I guess we'll have to settle for your horses."

"I don't have any stables or horses," said Mr. Clark, earnestly and honestly. "Here's the way such a setup works. You make your bid and you get your contract. Then you sublet the work to men who supply their own equipment, horses and wagons and gear and such, part-time farmers mostly in my case, who work for day wages."

The man in the candy-stripe shirt began hitting the hammerspur of his big nickel gun with the heel of his left hand, back and forth, back and forth. He did this five times and the room pounded with the explosions of the heavy cartridges. Joey's father went out of the kitchen chair, dead, to the floor in a sickening rumple of clothes. Joey couldn't see his face, but he could see pooling blood.

"I don't know when I ever made an easier thousand dollars," said the man.

"Divided by three," said the elderly man. His eyes seemed lidless.

The man in the ornate belt said, "Let's move." He said it like an order.

Scarcely were they gone than Joey was bending over the unresponsive thing on the floor. He hardly realized it when he left the house, ghostly in the pines, the towering Big

10

Horns behind it molten yellow and dusty green in the midmorning sun, and numbly made his way to Rush Ledderman's.

Joey's father had been the nominal head of the operation, but Rush Ledderman was the operation itself, body and soul. He could do, and did, everything from curing horses of poll-evil to precision supervising of difficult grading. He was an awkward looking man, thinnish, big knuckled, and with hot deep blue eyes. He didn't look like a teamster, and wasn't, and didn't look like a cowhand, and wasn't.

He was thirty-three years old and had spent a good third of his life in jails and penitentiaries.

He had started out as a gunfighter and fill-in lawman, like many, had found the line pretty hard to walk, at times actually nonexistent, and had ended up like others as a drifting professional gunman, for sale in range wars, satisfaction guaranteed, eventually outlawed and classed criminal and dangerous. In those days he thought the world was against him. He recognized fairness and justice for the first time in a judge who told him the man he'd killed was a heap worse than he was, and didn't sentence him to hanging.

When the jail gates opened the last time, he came home here. While everybody was friendly enough to him, nobody seemed to have an honest job for him, not just now. The other kind of a job he knew he could find easy, but he no longer wanted the other kind.

Then the government opened this road project: to repair, mend, and bring back to its original condition the pike that ran its eighty-seven miles from the county seat, Pelburg, through some of the most varied country in Montana, mountainsides, high meadows, rockfalls, wide rich grassland ranches, to the fort, Fort Justin. And put an advertisement in newspapers saying bids were being taken.

Rush sought out Rann Clark, who had been a friend of his father's and was now a retired stockman, and together they slaved over estimates.

The estimate they finally worked out was bedrock low, foolproof, unbeatable, and they knew it. The profit was small, but there was a decent fair profit. They were careful not to get hoggish.

Then, just at this stage, it came to their attention a fact they should have realized from the beginning: the government, at least the local spokesman for it, didn't relish granting contracts to prison-fresh felons, and Rann Clark did a shockingly generous thing.

He submitted the bid in his own name, won it, and turned the thing over to Rush, refusing to take a penny out of it.

When Rush at first declined, Joey's father persuaded him. "It's about yore last chance to turn back into a human again," he said. "Take it."

Rush took it, took it and did a crazy-perfect job of it: people noticed. He half killed himself from exhaustion. People noticed this, and began to respect him.

When he had a job and community respect, he proposed to a childhood sweetheart who still loved him and had no objection to wedding him. He built a little cottage just like she wanted, with trellises and roses, and laid the groundwork for a family. For the first time in his life, he realized that that was where happiness really was, in foolishness like this.

He gave his stag-handled gun, which had saved his life so many times, and had gotten him into so much trouble, to his wife and told her to hide it. In fact, he told her exactly where to hide it. He said, "Amelia, hide this in your dresser drawer with that sachet and all them underthings of yours. God knows I'll never find it there. And it'll be handy for you if you need it. And a woman ought to always have a gun handy. I'm through with it, but you never know when *you'll* need it."

She was small, birdlike, always very serious, a daughter of a storekeeper he had met at a dance in Pelburg when he was a boy. She said, "I needed it yesterday. To hammer in the catches when I was hanging curtain rods."

He flinched, but didn't reprove her. "Better

always unload it before you hammer with it. Know how to unload it?"

"Yes," she said. "But I don't like to. Anymore than I like to set a mousetrap."

"I'd advise it," he said patiently.

"If you say so," she agreed. "There's certain things a man knows best, just like there's certain things a woman knows best. How would you bake an apple pie?"

"Rim-fire or center-fire?" he asked.

When Joey came almost sightless-eyed and taut-cheeked up the little brick walk to Ledderman's side porch, he was sitting on a milking stool, beeswax and a loop of twine on his knee, a palming needle in his hand, repairing a piece of harness for one of his farmer-teamsters. A good gunfighter managed to continue to exist for two reasons: a fast draw, and an eerie genius in sensing human emotions. You not only had to beat your opponent out of your leather, but you had to sense the very instant he had reached his crisis. Everybody talked about a fast draw, but that mind reading part was as important, maybe twice as important. Rush had put away his gun, but he could never put away this intuition, this gauging of human anger, or anxiety, or distress, and he knew this boy had not only been shocked but seriously shocked. He hooked up a nearby chair, toe in its rung, and said, "Sit down."

Joey crumpled into it.

"Now what?" asked Rush, in a gentle but commanding voice.

The boy came out of his half coma and told him.

For ten minutes, Rush questioned him. He questioned him in that same steady voice that permitted no hysteria or panic, and the boy found himself answering, fully.

"You'll stay here with Amy," Rush said finally. "She'll take care of the funeral arrangements and such. Later, we hope, you'll live with us."

"What do you mean?" said the boy. "I don't want you to leave me. Are you going to leave me? Right now?"

"You bet I am. Right now."

Rage churned in him so that for an instant his face terrified the boy.

He saw what he had done, and composed himself. Casually, he said, "The man with the Mexican emblem on his belt. How did you know it was the Mexican emblem?"

"My grandpa fought in the Texas war. I got a Mexican flag on my bedroom wall."

"Amy's having fried chicken in about an hour," said Rush.

The boy looked horrified. "I couldn't eat nothing. It's like I got maggots in my stomach."

"Then she'll fix you a glass of hot milk with a little salt and butter. Drink it for me. Promise?"

15

"I'll try to, but I don't see how I can."

"That's not good enough."

"Then I will. I promise. Who were these fellers?"

"Trash. Gun-trash. For every real gunman in this new country they's a hundred gun-trash."

"Why did they do it?"

"I don't know. But it wasn't for the strongbox or horses. They knew about you, didn't they? So they came already informed and must have knowed there were no horses or strongbox."

He went into the house and returned wearing his gun, with Amy at his side. She was unexcited.

She said, "How long do you think you'll be gone?"

"I don't know," said Rush. "There ain't no way of telling. I'll pick up a pack mule at Mr. Guffy's."

He told her to see John Sutton and tell him to run things while he was gone. Sutton was a sort of straw boss, a small subcontractor who worked five teams himself, and who could, and on occasion did, act as substitute paymaster and general supervisor. He was a reliable man.

"You'll need a pack mule?" asked his wife. "You'll be gone that long?"

"Right now I'd say yes," said Rush. "I'd place those killers as wanderers, and I might have to look a little."

"You going to find them and bring them back?" asked Joey.

"Well, anyways, I'm going to find them," said Rush evasively.

Shortly, they watched him vanish on his fine bay over a rise of grassland.

After a long pause, the boy said, "Asking Mr. Guffy for the loan of a pack mule, when it's knowed everywhere how Mr. Guffy hates him . . ."

"I have an idea if Rush asks him, Mr. Guffy will lend it to him," said Mrs. Ledderman. "Rush has different manners in asking for different things. Different voices, and different kinds of smiles, to suit different occasions, you might say."

"You know," said the boy, "I believe, and will always believe, that it was Mr. Guffy himself who paid those men to kill my father. He hated my father more than he hates Rush."

"Then I pity him," said Mrs. Ledderman. "And what Rush leaves, I'll take care of myself."

II

THE ROAD, called locally the Military Road, was considered important back along the Eastern seaboard and other such places as necessary for what they called "the opening of the West." First came the fort, then Pelburg with its railroad as a sort of immigrant staging center, and then the road between them.

Some of the inhabitants of that eighty-seven mile stretch it traversed liked it, and found it a convenience for getting into town to market; some, for multiple reasons, such as that it and its traffic scarred their rangeland, yelled against it.

The man who objected most was John Guffy, a moderately sizable cattleman in the valley. The headwaters of the streams which gave the valley its lush grazing were high in the mountains. He claimed—and managed to fire up a few of his neighbors in the same belief—that the road, elevated in places, acted as a barrier and affected the mountainside watershed, maybe drying some stream channels, maybe creating new ones. He was a bullheaded, brutal man, brutal to his barn-stock, to his dogs, to his wife, and neither Rush nor Joey's father put it past him to ambush an unarmed man, say a teamster, if the mood seized him. All this despite the fact the road predated him.

Things got so bad at one time that the government sent an engineer to explain. The roadside was ditched, according to customary government specifications, and drains were adjusted to lead the water properly from these side ditches: this had all been carefully calculated. Culverts were carefully placed, and carefully kept clean. The watershed was in no way influenced by the road.

Nevertheless, Guffy's obsession grew, steadily approaching a climax, and became an ugly and insane thing directed personally against Rann Clark and Rush.

Instantly, when Rush had heard of the murder, he had thought of Guffy. It was like him to protect himself by getting someone else, and his mind would run to such trash to do it. But it wasn't like him to pay a thousand dollars when he could do it himself through a window at night for the price of a shotgun shell.

Guffy's ranch house itself was modest, constructed in the old fashion, and belied the considerable spread it controlled. It was of two medium-sized log cabins separated by the roofed breezeway or "dog run." The logs in the cabins were twisted and knotty, for this particular piece of country was almost treeless and the builder had to use whatever he could get, and the logs were chinked with red-tinted scoria, or volcanic dirt. The roof was scoria, roughly piled on raw hides. When Rush rode up and dismounted, Guffy was sitting in the dog run on a thong bottomed chair, just sitting there, shooing off swarming flies which somehow seemed mightily attracted to him and his greasy clothes.

He was an oxlike man with a pouchy face, slovenly. His glass-splinter eyes were almost entirely embedded in sacs of purplish flesh and his mouth was tight and ruthless looking. He stared through Rush as though Rush didn't exist.

Leisurely, Rush glanced around, a practice once automatic with him, now almost forgotten. There were ranch buildings, sheds, a corral, but nothing else, no one in sight. High on the mountainside, to the left of the house and above it, was the road, a snowy white line.

"Where's everybody?" asked Rush conversationally. "This is a slack season. There should be hands in sight."

"They ain't no slack season on the GG," said Guffy. "They's always something to be did. They're out on the place, hither and yon." Hatefully, he added, "And you can move on, as far as I'm concerned. You know as well as I do you're unwelcome here."

"I come for three reasons," said Rush impassively. "To borrow a pack mule—"

"You expect to borrow a pack mule, or anything else, off'n me?" said Guffy and laughed. He

20

laughed mirthlessly, simply baring his teeth, like a dog snarls on a fight.

"To borrow a pack mule," continued Rush, "to bring you some news, and to ask you a question or two."

Guffy brushed flies and looked entirely uninterested.

Rush said, "The news is that Rann Clark was gunned down unarmed at his breakfast table this morning."

After a long, long interval, Guffy said, "Well, it happens to the best of us."

"And to the worst of us, too," said Rush heavily. "Which is always a good thing to remember."

Guffy said, "I wonder who it was that done it? Was it robbery?"

"It wasn't robbery, it was murder pure and simple," said Rush. "And we got a pretty good idea just who done it. Three men. One was oldish, one was just, well, ordinary, and the other wore a red and white shirt and pants that was out at the knees. They was well seen and well described by a certain party."

"By who?" asked Guffy.

"By my wife," said Rush.

"Your wife!" said Guffy startled.

"My wife," said Rush placidly. He couldn't let it get out that the boy had witnessed it. "And others."

"How come she to see 'em?" asked Guffy.

"They stopped by my place and asked how to get to you," said Rush.

"Not me," said Guffy, aghast. "Not me, Rush, and that's the truth. I never seen nor heard of no fellers like them!"

"All I know is what she told me," said Rush. "And she wouldn't lie to me."

"Listen, Rush," said Guffy, shocked. "They didn't come and didn't have no reason to come. And I been right here all day and swear I didn't see 'em!"

"I may be gone for a few days," said Rush. "I'm going to see if I can find them. If anything happens to my wife while I'm gone, I'm going to hold you responsible personally. I don't say you have anything to do with this, but I'm just telling you."

"You can't do that!" said Guffy, sweating now, his eyes popping open. "I ain't in this thing at all, and you don't have no right to try to bring me in. You can't—"

"I'll need a pack mule," said Rush.

"And I've got a dandy," said Guffy. "You'll need supplies, too." He got up briskly. "Just wait a minute."

He disappeared, and returned leading a pack mule, little and grizzled and strong, lashed with traveling gear.

"Thank you kindly," said Rush. "That's the one I had in mind." He mounted his bay. "One thing more."

"Of course, nacherly, certainly," said Guffy. "What's that?"

"The road. I've personally took it on myself to inspect the ten few miles from here to Pelburg while it's under repair. I'd appreciate it if you'd sort of keep an eye on it for me."

"I'm a working stockman," said Guffy, harried. "I don't have much spare time. I'm sorry."

As though he hadn't heard him, Rush said, "There'll be a regular boss on the job, so just see everything's going right. Be sure they're raking the old bed well. These parts of the old bed should have a rise of not more than three inches to the center. The new layers go on in three inch layers, then after a little traffic, more raking, then another layer of crushed rock. You don't need to worry about the catch-waters or culverts, or drains, or the masonry of the sidewalls, where they're needed. The boss is better in all them things. Just let 'em see you riding by, studyin' things, that's about all I do."

"All right, I'll do it," said Guffy, suddenly reversing himself. "Whenever I can find time, in fact I'll make time. You know why?"

"Why?"

"Because I always wanted to be friendly with you, Rush. If you'd jest have let me."

Rush rode off with his pack mule. He didn't bother to say goodbye.

He didn't really want the road inspected. He just wanted his say-so over Guffy.

When he had described the gunmen to Guffy he hadn't mentioned the gunbelt with the eagle on it. For the time being, he was keeping this gunbelt to himself. It was the barb on the hook he hoped to snag the men by.

Unless he was sadly mistaken, he had owned that very gunbelt once.

With an eye like an eagle for a straight line and the shortest distance, passing through some mighty fine grass and some mighty fine Guffy cattle, it was just after sunset, the time of the day Rush had been raised to call dusk-dark, when he rode into Pelburg. It was a good-sized town now, as towns went out here, all dust from passing freight wagons and bawling from cow pens and gongs and steam from locomotives; a good many of its inhabitants could remember the daybreak yell of marauding Indians in prairie cabins, but most couldn't. Talk in barbershops was mainly about the Chicago exchange and St. Louis market prices for beef.

Go eight miles out of town, though, and into the scrub, and your life was just as good as you were, and no better. Everything but guns and ammunition went back twenty years and more. Guns and ammunition were almost always up to the split second as modern as you could get. Many a hardscrabble rancher's wife sorted

24

buttons by the light of a crude homemade candle while a rifle of Winchester's newest and finest production gleamed spotless on buckhorns over the door.

Now, in the dusk-dark, the town looked peaceful and shabby, though Rush knew it actually to be hair-trigger and prosperous. He went through the business section of fancy brick and frame, violet gray as twilight rolled in, some of the buildings already showing weak nightlights; he gave the courthouse and jail a hard stare, for he had established bad friendships with them when he was a boy, and turned his mare into an alley by the Gem Saloon. He passed the saloon's backdoor with its rubbish and rats, and continued onward until he came to a shed-like shanty. A long board above the door said, H. TATE. I BUY, SELL, SWAP ANYTHING. HORSES, GUNS, SADDLES, DOGS, MOTHER-IN-LAWS, ANYTHING. Here Rush got out of his saddle, hitched his mare to a wagon-wheel, and knocked out the signal: three, three, one.

From within, a jolly voice called, "Customer, enter at your own risk."

Rush swung open the creaking door and entered.

Inside, the room was small and grubby, patch-work walled with salvaged packing box tops and sides of pine. The only light came from a squat sooty lamp on a packing box table. There was a built-in cot in a corner with a dirty USA blanket hanging half to the dirt floor, two ice cream chairs with wire backs, and a potbellied stove for heating and whatever Tate called cooking.

Tate, a pinched little man with a leather bald head and a puckered-in mouth, sat at his table putting a new edge on a rusty circle-saw with a rusty file. "When I get through," he said, flicking his eyes up at his visitor, and back to his work, "she'll sell for at least five simoleenens. But I won't sell her. I'll trade her, maybe for a broke down wagon."

Rush said, "And the wagon for a racehorse, and the horse for a herd o' horses, and then a mess of other things, and then the mess for the state of Montana."

"I don't want the state of Montana. And for that matter, who does?" said Tate, and laid down his saw and file. The polite introductory conversation over, he said quietly, "If you've came to bring me the news, Rush, I already seen the body at the undertakers and paid it my respects."

They had been mighty close friends, Rush and Clark and Tate.

"When I got finished with jail," said Rush, "when Rann Clark went out of his way to help me, I came to you and sold you all my previous belongings. Recall?"

Tate glanced at the stag-handled gun at Rush's side, and glanced away. "Almost all, yes, I recall."

"Amongst them was a Mexican gunbelt with an eagle on it. Recall?"

"I recall."

"Who did you sell it to?"

"I didn't sell it. I give it away, you could say. Give it to the stableman at the Congress livery stable. In trade for a paltry colt give to him by a drunk rancher."

"He still got it?"

"Had it less than a week and traded it to a gamblin' lucky emigrant bent on passin' through."

"Where was this emigrant headed for?"

"I said *bent* on passin' through. He never got a chance to tell anybody. A man that owns a belt like that gets a seizure, nacherly, to wear it. He put it on and in about seven minutes it had two .45 holes in it."

"What I'm trying to find out is where can I find it now?"

"Maybe in Canada, maybe back home in Mexico. The man that shot him took it. And sold it on the spot to a railroad brakeman standing there with a schooner of beer. Brakemen travel, and see a passel o' people. Why you so interested in it?"

Rush described the three men who had murdered Rann Clark. "One of them wore that belt, or another like it," he ended.

"How do you know what they looked like?"

asked Tate, with concentrated interest. "Did you see them?"

"They were seen," said Rush, poker-faced. He could tell no one about Joey, even this good friend.

Tate nodded in agreement. "I don't know what got into me to ask. If you'd wanted to have told, you've have told."

"If they'd come once, they'd sure as hell come again, and I can't go light and easy with another party's life," said Rush.

"I'll make you a little swap," said Tate. "You better say yes."

"Yes."

"Here's your end o' the swap. Answer me this: they'll never be hanged, by nobody, no time, will they? You're looking for 'em right now, for personal reasons?"

"Every man has his debts."

"That's sufficient. Here's my end of the swap. Maybe I can help you. You're on the wrong track complete. I know these men. I ain't never laid eyes on them, but I've heard o' them in my business, the way a careful listener does. They ain't gunmen, like you think. Oh, they've doubtless slew their share of the halt and the blind, but that ain't actually their trade. Cows is their trade."

"Stealing cows?"

"I shore as hell don't mean raising 'em."

"Where can I find them?"

"When they came down here like they did, they was a long way from their general stamping grounds. They work the high prairie north, between the Musselshell and the Bear Paws, where there's a lot of new stockman that know more about their Boston bank accounts and such than they do about a cow or a cow-thief. I disremember the names of these men—if I ever heard their names—but they favor hanging out at a little hen scratch of a settlement on the Musselshell, just south of where it V's into the Missouri, a place that goes by the name of Lister. Now that was the swap. Here comes the boot."

Among traders, Rush knew, the boot was the little extra something sometimes added.

Cautiously, Rush said, "What?"

"It's that I go along with you. You may not believe it, but I can ride a little better than most, and can shoot passably well, all things considered."

"If you say so, I believe it," declared Rush. "But I'd better do this alone."

"You'll be in their territory, not yours, and amongst their friends, not yours."

"I guess I'll just have to take it as it comes," said Rush amiably.

Tate went to a ragged coat hanging from a nail on the wall, took out a folded paper and spread it on the packing box table. It was a map of Montana.

"Now here's us here, Pelburg," he said, touching the map with his broken thumbnail. "And the railroad. The railroad goes west, like you see. Up here, northwest a little less than a couple of hundred miles, is Lister. Here. The map don't show it because it's scarcely nothin'. What I'd say is you do this: take the railroad here at Pelburg, as far west as Jennington, here, get off and go the rest of the way, almost due north, to Lister, about fifteen miles. That way, when you get to Lister, you'll arrive a little before them, if they hit straight for home, and they will. Bein' there when they come in might be an advantage. Do you follow me, and agree?"

"I believe I do," said Rush.

"The thing is, when you get to Lister you might not run into them face to face, and might have to run 'em down. Fellers like them does a heap of riding. You may need a pack animal. If I was you I'd pick it up in advance on my way in, at Jennington."

"I got a pack animal. Joe Guffy's fine little gray mule. He loaned it to me."

"Loaned it to you?" said Tate. "I thought he hated you!"

"So did I. But it seems now that all along that was just his way of trying to be friendly."

"You can say this for him," said Tate. "When he's friendly, he shore don't overdo it."

30

III

THE FIRST THING Rush did when the train stopped at Jennington was to watch while they unloaded his bay, and check her to see how she had stood the trip; she seemed absolutely okay, unnervous, and looked as though she had been well handled. He saddled her as they put off Guffy's pack mule. The next thing he did was go to a general-merchandise store and take on traveling grub. He knew a little more about manhunts than most, and knew you could never exactly tell not only where one might end but just when one might start. He might run into his quarry right here on the streets of Jennington, for instance, and they get away from him, and a long, long trip might follow. He should be days ahead of them, but he had no guarantee of that. Logically, the big chase should begin in Lister, and he could get his supplies there, but it could be he'd never even see Lister.

The town of Jennington seemed at first about like any other Montana cattle market and exchange point, another bead of population that had accumulated on the string which was the railroad, slightly smaller than Rush's hometown, Pelburg, but farther west and a heap wilder, even to the eye. One thing the people who didn't know them didn't realize was that the high prairies were pounded and battered ceaselessly by winds, winter and summer, and the town's buildings, while not really old as old went, already looked decrepit and dust blasted.

For that matter, the buildings themselves, even in the business section, weren't much to brag about, just flimsy structures of raw planking, or crinkled with bone-dry whitewash, or showing wood grain through over-thinned brown or green paint, just somewhere to eat, or sleep, or get in out of the sun to wash the soil from your throat with a mug of beer, or mortgage a few cows, maybe nonexistent, or buy a new string for your banjo.

Rush bought a can of tomatoes, took it out into a slice of shade, opened it with his jackknife, and drank off the gullet-cleansing juice. Then, munching the pulp, which was like fruit to him, he looked around. One thing jails had taught him was to see a town differently from most people, to see it in layers. A sixth sense, plus an indefinable feeling from many of the shop and saloon fronts, told him that Jennington had a heavy, and an extra heavy layer of jail-fodder. And jail-fodder, he knew, came in great variety. Here in Jennington, he was certain, you could hire anything from a lightning gun artist to a man who could re-ear-crop a herd of stolen cavalry horses for a sergeant who happened to need a little capital to finance a deluxe desertion. The town, obviously, was a funnel mouth for outlaws from the wild north—just as this Lister place must be an outpost of it. His three men could have collected their thousand dollars here, or up at Lister. It was a toss-up. He tied up his animals, securely.

There was a long, low two-story hotel, glaring white in the sun. A sign above its ground floor door said, BUELL HOUSE: above it a second sign said, COURTHOUSE. Steep steps led from the sidewalk upward. Rush passed it by, and hoped he never saw it again. He strolled slowly, sizing things up. He'd seen meaner towns, but not many.

The cheap storefronts and packed earth underfoot threw off as much heat as an incandescent horseshoe just out of the forge.

He was fumbling in the sweaty breast pocket of his open beaded vest for his Bull Durham sack when a voice said, "They put one on us for sure today, Albert. The temperature is a hundred and two!" It was a careless voice, but vaguely strangled and unnatural. Rush had heard a voice on that order once, from a man who had got hit in the gullet with an ax handle. He turned.

He had never laid eyes on the man before.

The man said, "Oh, excuse me. You're not Albert."

Rush came to a halt. "No, I'm not. And I doubt if you even know anyone named Albert." He spoke good-naturedly, and added, "What do you think you're leading up to?"

They were standing before a narrow window fronting that was a little fancier than its neighbors. Its glass was painted bright green inside and topped with a broad goldleaf stripe. A small dignified gold name said, Thos. L. Grayville.

The man himself, standing just outside his door, was slim, tanned, well-dressed in town style. In the hollow of each cheek he had a scar about the size of a thumbnail, glossy white with scar tissue. "Caught a Cheyenne bullet straight through both cheeks once," said the man. "Makes me talk like a frog." A bubble of saliva came and went in a corner of his lips. "Sometimes it makes me bubble."

He was so insensitive about it that Rush grinned. Grinned, but didn't relax. He wondered how many times this very speech had been used to make people relax.

"All right, Mr. Grayville," said Rush. "I have a feeling it's me you want to talk to, not any Albert. What do you want to say?"

"I'm not Mr. Grayville, I'm Mr. Hankinson," said the man, blowing no bubble now. "Mr. Grayville's assistant. And now that we're getting along so well, I'll tell there is no Mr. Grayville. I put that up when I started in business, thinking it would be useful. But I don't need it."

Rush was interested. He thought the man

34

was running some sort of sidewalk thimblerig, but anything at all connected with this town interested him.

Rush asked, "Just what is your business?"

"I'm a purchasing agent for a St. Louis stockyard," said Hankinson.

"Business good?" asked Rush.

"Business is fine," said Hankinson. "You see, I'm known as a man who will buy a herd sight unseen."

"You must be a gift of God to a lot of ranchers, if they're like some I've known," said Rush. "With all the big jaws, stags, runts, cripples and other culls on these ranges, just begging to be fobbed off, how do you stay in business?"

"For one thing, I've got my own personal business. I'm a speculator."

"Speculator?"

"A rancher knows his herd, and studies it. I know the market, and study it. If I figure the market due to go way up, and it does, I make a big killing."

"And if it goes down?" said Rush dryly.

"I'm very rarely riding on its coattails," said Hankinson.

Rush thought this over. Finally, he said, "Even then it wouldn't work. Not with culls and garbage."

"Somehow, I never seem to handle any culls and garbage."

"And how do you manage that, with sight unseen?" asked Rush, knowing very well he was on a conversational path that had been carefully blazed out for him to follow with just these responses.

Hankinson dodged that one. He said, "Did I see you just hitch up that pack mule and that big bay yonder?"

Rush nodded.

"Where are you headed?" asked Hankinson.

"How do I know?" said Rush truthfully.

"I've told you my name," declared Hankinson. "But I didn't seem to catch yours."

"I've used so many," said Rush, again truthfully, "that I scarcely know which one to choose for you. How about Pryor?"

This seemed not only satisfactory to Hankinson, but exactly the sort of response he had hoped for.

He said, "You asked me how I manage, and I'll tell you. I think you are the kind of man I trust. First off, that sight unseen is really just a kind of slogan, a kind of business getter, you might say. I never bought a thing in my life I didn't know exactly what it was beforehand. I listen to talk about herds and, if I have to, go and look things over myself in a kind of accidental way. But mostly, certain gentlemen like yourself, ambling here and there, tip me off when they see something. When they come to a telegraph, they notify me. Later, I see that they get paid well for their trouble. Would you like to take on such a job for me in your drifting?"

"I don't see why not," said Rush.

"Just send the message, *The major's mare has foaled,* to me here. And sign it with the name of the ranch brand and county where you saw them. Like *N-Box-N, Stratton County.*"

And later, if there should be any cows missing from N-Box-N they won't be after me first of all, thought Rush. *Oh my no, not at all.*

Hankinson gave Rush a slow, hard inspection. He saw an awkward man, coatless, shirt-sleeved, with sultry blue eyes almost blue-black. He wore denims old and soft, and an Indian beaded vest, flapping open. The beads had been strung to make crude pictures of horses and men. The little squarish men and the little squarish horses told the story of a massacre of twelve Irish troopers by a Sioux war band, but neither Rush nor Hankinson could translate it. Rush, on occasion, had seen Indians smile at it happily and had put it down to just good Indian craftmanship.

"Why not?" said Rush. "I'll do it."

They held their conversation until a passerby got beyond earshot.

"I'm just interested in the very finest cattle, you understand," said Hankinson. "The kind of cows that when you look one in the face your mouth waters because all you think of is delicious marbled rib roast."

"When do I get paid, and where?" asked Rush.

"That I can't tell you at the moment. When, or where, or how much. But it'll come, and it'll be a mighty pleasant surprise."

"And if it never comes?"

"It'll come. But I'll always be here, and you can always come back and take it out on me."

"Anything else?" asked Rush.

"Yes. I'd like it better if there hadn't been any rustling scares thereabouts lately. Rustling scares upset a cow's elements, and I don't want to buy any cows with upset elements."

"That's reasonable," said Rush. "I'll keep that in mind." He gestured affably, and walked away. He felt funny. Not scared, but funny. He knew that despite all that St. Louis purchasing agent talk, and speculator talk, he had wedged himself into a big cow stealing ring.

His bay greeted him with a whinny as he approached, and he answered with a soft soothing whistle. Guffy's mule craned its neck straight upward, bared gigantic teeth, and cut loose with a bray that sounded like a saw rasping through a log with a nail in it. They were restless after their train ride and wanted to get going, anywhere, as long as their knee joints were working. He pattcd his bay, almost lost a hand patting the mule, mounted and set off. An hour later, they were well out of town, headed due north, to Lister.

He moved at a leisurely pace, for it was late afternoon and his plan was to camp that night and get into Lister next day. This gave him plenty of time to think. The problem was why three men, not even professional gunmen, but flotsam and jetsam cattle thieves—for he was certain that was what they must be—should travel over two hundred miles to kill Rann Clark.

An ugly answer kept pushing itself at him and he kept rejecting it: that there was some kind of a link between the four of them. Rann Clark had been a cattleman once, true, and you might say there was a link there, cows and cows, but he had long retired and when he was slaughtered owned not a single calf.

So Rush's duty now, as he saw it, had more than doubled. It was not only to find the men but to learn why they had come. Clark was almost a hero to him. The answer might destroy all his illusions and leave him heartsick, but he would never again rest until he knew.

The country he was approaching was becoming truly out-country. The grass continued, in shallow swales and low rises, and seemed to become more lush, but humanity became sparse, approaching the vanishing point, it seemed, and it was rare indeed when he saw a cabin or a speck of a distant rider against the setting sun. He spent the night in a belt of alders along a tiny freshwater stream.

. . .

By noon next day, the country had changed almost into another world. It had started with the grass thinning, at first in little patches of sere parched earth spotting it, and then again altered, the earth patches increasing in number and size and the grass giving away to tussocks of brambles and wild honeysuckle. Midmorning, the tussocks had given away to long hogback hummocks at first dry and crusty, then, by degrees, showing dampness and finally stagnant water in the depressions between them. Now, some distance away, he saw a density of trees and undergrowth, interwoven and looped with wrist-thick vines of wild grape, and knew he was approaching a river, the Musselshell certainly. The sloughs between the hummocks stank with the putrefaction of their rotting leaf-covered bottoms, and their sides were sometimes thick with the brownish earth-colored backs of poisonous watersnakes, dozing.

He knew he was headed right, and on a trail of sorts, for he followed a winding course along the hummock ridges which now and then showed the decomposed stub ends of small ax-cut logs telling him this had once been a corduroy road. It had never been much of a road and things, neglected, rotted quickly in this oppressive mosquito-laden humidity. When he got to the trees, the road, scarcely wagon-wide, showed up in better shape and became a tunnel through the low-hanging foliage.

Then, before he knew it, the trees were behind him and he was in Lister, in the center of it.

The town, or settlement really, as Tate had called it, was composed of a couple of dozen buildings strung out in a ragged line, facing the river. Rush had come in from the back, and just about in the center of the line. Once apparently, from the corduroy road, people had expected this to be a good location, a sort of river port to the new grasslands. Maybe it actually had been for a while, but the railroad at Jennington had cut its throat and left it to die. Behind it now was only the dense river growth and before it, in a shallow incline, was the shore. The water of the river, now at its seasonal low, was glass green, breaking into froth around white rock shards, and the long slope of the shore was dried clay and silt, cracked into curling crazy patterns in the sun's oven.

Rush emerged from between two of the buildings, to the front. One of the buildings had crudely printed across its front, I SELL GRUB & BUY PELTS. The other, in six foot white letters, said only, BEER.

Three men sat on a bench in a narrow strip of lavender shadow before this building. One of them, with an unshaved, bloated face, wore denim pants out at the knees and a red and white candy-stripe shirt. One of them was an old lizard-

41

faced man with skeletal hands. The third man, the man at the end, in faded khaki and with a crimson silk neckerchief, wore Rush's Mexican carved leather gunbelt.

Both Tate and Rush had thought the train would give him a good headstart on them, that it would be days before they would ride in. But they had simply done what Rush had done: taken the train. And an earlier one at that.

Rush said, "Howdy," as he dismounted and hitched. But none of the three acknowledged his presence. None of them spoke a word, or so much as lifted a casual thumb in greeting.

Even the meanest outlaw would have ordinarily responded. In fact, he would have made a point of doing so.

Rush walked past them and into the building.

The most important thing now was to find out why they had done it.

He appraised them from the corner of his eye as he passed them.

They were dead men, nothing could save them, but in their mood of ignorant bliss, were self-important and complacent. Each of them had three hundred dollars in his pocket, didn't he?

IV

THE ROOM WAS small, square, and walled with silvery driftwood logs. It had no windows, for windows were expensive and unnecessary and afforded only such fripperies as pleasant sunlight and healthy fresh air. The place smelled like toadstools and earthworms and beery malt. A man stood behind a counter by a lamp, working on a funny looking gun which lay on the counter before him. Rush had seen several guns exactly like it before, but not many. It was monstrous. Its barrel seemed about six feet long and its muzzle-mouth looked about the size of an empty pork-and-bean can. It was the gun of a certain type of so-called "duck-hunter" who murdered ducks for the market. The number of ducks that could be murdered by one of its single discharges was almost unbelievable. These ducks would then be dumped into barrels, carted to the railroad, and end up under a cut-glass chandelier in some elegant Eastern hotel dining room.

The man himself was more beast than human to Rush's eye, liver-lipped, ferret-eyed, small-headed but massive-necked. He looked up, finished what he was doing, and said expressionlessly, "We don't see many strangers. What did you have in mind?"

"A bottle of beer," said Rush.

"Bottle or glass?"

"Bottle," repeated Rush. If it came in a bottle it was theoretically factory sanitary.

"Bottle it is, then," said the man. And put a bottle on the counter. It was a square thin bottle about fourteen inches high and when he opened it for Rush a slimy yellow foam erupted from it.

"I said beer," said Rush. "Not home brew in a horse liniment bottle."

"There's some that prefer my brew to the Milwaukee product," said the man. "Or are you just trying to get my dander up? That'll be twenty-five cents."

Benignly, Rush paid the outrageous price, and drank the fluid in one long gulp. It tasted about half grain alcohol.

"Like it?" said the barman. "How about another?"

"Later," said Rush.

"How soon later?"

"Well, one thing for sure. Not until I stop hearing these moose-calls and snare drums and tom-toms."

"Travelin'?" said the barman, now inclined to be sociable.

"That's about it," said Rush. "Which reminds me. I got a pack mule and my mare outside, and seen three hungry looking boys looking them over. Are my animals safe, would you say?"

"Sure they're safe," said the barman. "Those boys are long-time friends o' mine and as honest as the day is long!"

Long-time friends. So the barman must be either in the circle, or at least on intimate terms with it.

Rush said, "How near is the nearest telegraph?"

"Jennington," said the barman. "A seizure come over you to send a telegram?"

"To Jennington, as a matter of fact," said Rush. "To a man named Hankinson."

The barman picked up his enormous duck-killing contraption, squinted down its barrel, and returned it to the counter. "I've heard of this Mr. Hankinson. Cattle purchaser for some St. Louis yards."

"That's him," said Rush. "Seems like he's got this friend, a major, who raises these thorough-bred trotters and Mr. Hankinson has always favored one in particular. I want to telegraph him that the major's mare has foaled."

"I know several retired majors that has gone in for horse breedin'," said the barman conversationally. "What county does this one live in? And what's the name of his ranch?"

"The telegram was for Mr. Hankinson," said Rush affably, but reproachfully.

The three grubby killers from outside came through the door, into the lamplit room.

They entered in a sort of loose triangle, the man

45

with the Mexican belt in the fore, the lizard-faced oldster slightly behind him and a little to his left, the man in the red and white shirt to the right of this one, and also a little behind. Their guns were in their holsters. Rann Clark, in his kitchen, had had no gun at all. Now they had nothing on their minds except maybe a drink of that strange malt-brandy beer.

Leisurely, Rush drew his stag-handled gun and killed all three of them. He didn't make it a gunfight, he made it an execution. He went about it like he'd been told they shot a line of walking wild turkeys in the Big Smokies. The last one first, so the ones in front couldn't see him go down and stampede. He shot the man in the striped shirt carefully, once, dead center just above the bridge of his nose, and the old man through the heart. He got a small surprise from the man in the lead, the man in the belt, who turned out to have mighty quick reflexes and had to get off three extra quick ones to finish him.

The last cartridge he saved for the barman if he should need it, wheeling to face him.

He didn't need it. The barman was grinning, as the old-timers used to say, like a cat eating paste.

"For a minute there," he said. "It sounded like a railroad crew beating on an empty box car with twelve pound sledges. Did you have a reason for all that, or was time jest hangin' heavy on your hands?"

46

"I had a reason," said Rush curtly.

"Would you consider it personal if I inquired what was this reason?"

Rush said tonelessly, "I was in Waco, Texas, once. It was a black rainy night and I was walking down an alley. A gun was pushed in my back. A man said, 'I fancy that belt,' and took it. I said, 'If I ever see you wearing it, I'll shoot on sight.' And that's what I just did. That's my Mexican gunbelt."

"If you say so, I'm not going to argue," said the barman. "But can you prove it?"

"There's a gentleman in Jennington can prove it for me. He knows me and my name. On the inside of the belt, on the rough side of the leather, it says Jim Pryor."

The barman unbuckled the belt, laid it out on the floor, and said, "Yes, here it is. Jim Pryor. You a friend of this Mr. Hankinson?"

"I work for him."

"Well, that puts a new light on matters. That makes us friends. He's got money in this place. What will we do with the bodies?"

"Me, nothing," said Rush. "I'm through with them." He pointed at them. "Search them."

The barman did, and came up with a total of about eight hundred dollars.

"Get rid of them and the money's yours," said Rush.

"Yes, Mr. Pryor, sir, I'll do it. And it ain't every

man that carries his buryin'-money on him. I'll take 'em upriver to a place I know of, tie some rocks to 'em, and drop 'em in a gar and crawfish hole." He paused, and added, "That's a mighty nice belt just to throw away."

"I think we'd better let the garfish decide that," said Rush.

"I guess you're right at that," said the barman. "By the way, there's law in this country now. Few and far between, but mighty sharp and unforgivin'. I'd say you'd best head for the Spencer Eakins outfit. Right now. Just to be on the safe side."

"Sounds like good advice," said Rush, having not the slightest idea what the man was talking about. "How do I get there the quickest way?"

With gestures and an economy of words, the barman directed him.

"But how can the law know, how can anybody know?"

"I won't tell. You can be shore o' that. But some folks will wonder, nacherly. They got some nasty pals, and maybe some of these pals knowed where they was today, where they went to and never come back from. Goodbye, Mr. Pryor. My name's Hayes."

The trail to the Spencer Eakins outfit, as laid out by the barman, began with the path on the near shore, the west shore of the Musselshell, and continued through an eight mile length of

48

canopied trees until Rush came to a great nest of birch stumps and two-foot saplings sprouting about its roots; here he was to turn into the foliage directly to his left. The shore trees would soon thin out and he would find himself in marsh grass. West would then still be his direction, with the sun directly before him. Shortly after he would hit rangeland. A few miles later, he would pass a deep bowl of grassland with the finger of a chimney from a burnt out cabin on its edge, continue toward the sun, and, if he took it easy, reach the Spencer Eakins ranch buildings about an hour or so later.

He came to the birch stumps, turned west as he had been directed, away from the river, passed through an area of marsh grass and cattails and reeds, and came abruptly out onto range, into as nice grass as he'd ever seen.

Nice grass, but, as far as he could tell, no cattle.

Soon he saw the chimney, like the black trunk of a charred tree in the distance against the red sky. As he came to it and passed the grassbowl, he glanced into the hollow and saw a puzzling sight. Here were cattle, a mess of them, fat and delicious looking.

But there was something more curious than that.

It wasn't trail droving season but this was sure as hell a trail herd, all settled on its bedground for the night, remuda, night-hawk, and everything, though it would be a good hour before twilight, just as though it were already dark.

He saw he was being observed when he rode up and hitched at the post-and-ring before the Spencer Eakins ranch house.

Now that the three killers, the three gun-trash, were dead they were as nothing to him, nothing. The thing that shook him, that dominated him, was Rann Clark's involvement with such depravity. Rann Clark's honor was his honor, and he had to know more about it.

He looked at the house with hard hostility.

Spencer Eakins himself answered Rush's knock. He turned out to be a hard-bitten man, furrow-cheeked, with as honest looking a pair of eyes as Rush had ever seen, and maybe a little too honest. When he turned his eyeballs into yours they became fixed, like they were bolted into place. The introductions in which the two men named themselves were quick and short. In the pause that followed, Rush said, "Hayes, Mr. Hankinson."

With no particular cordiality, he shook Rush's hand. "What can I do for you?"

"I'm looking for an overnight burrow," said Rush. "I got into a little mess-up back yonder with three men."

"Three? And they're chasin' you?"

"I don't want to put you out. I can move on."

"You ain't putting me out. Have you et?"

"No, sir. Not since morning."

"See that little building with them fellers going in? That's the cook house. You go in too and eat as much as you can swaller."

"Thank you," said Rush. "Can I leave my mount and pack mule here for the time being?"

Eakins nodded.

"If it's all the same with you," said Rush, "I won't sleep in the bunkhouse but camp out just a ways on the prairie. I'd like to come in for breakfast, though."

"Will I see you in the morning before you leave?"

"I wouldn't partake of a man's hospitality without thanking him and saying goodbye."

"Good enough," said Spencer Eakins. He withdrew into his house and closed his door.

Night had fallen by now. Rush made his way to the cook house, slipping his gun twice in its leather as he approached—not because he expected any trouble, but because it was an old precautionary habit he had once used that seemed to be returning to him. He stepped through the fan of yellow lamplight on the hard earth, and entered.

Up and down the sides of a table of unfinished pine sat about a dozen cowboys, gay, joking, eating ravenously. At the far end, at the head, sat their foreman, a big blocky man in a work shirt pooled with sweat under its armpits. There was nothing spurious or fraudulent about the men, any of them; they were workers and had just finished a hard day's labor. And what they ate would have bankrupted many a town restaurant, slices of beef as thick as your thumb, yams, pyramids of mashed potatoes floating with a gravy of chopped tongue and sweetbreads, biscuits the size of teacups sopping golden with butter.

Every eye turned on him as he appeared in the doorway.

He said, "Mr. Eakins said for me to come here and have some supper," and sat down.

The foreman said, "Make yourself at home. Pass the gentleman some hardware."

A gray enamel plate, bone-handled tableware appeared before him. He served himself and ate.

The light-hearted conversation resumed. Excluding him, but not maliciously excluding him. He was ignored because they thought he wanted to be ignored. He himself had given them their cue. He hadn't said, "I'm Jim Pryor (or Teton Slim, or whatever), Mr. Eakins sent me." He had left out any mention of his own name whatever. They took this to mean that he wanted to be left alone, and had seen solitary men before that wanted to be left alone, and sure as hell left them alone.

He finished his meal, eating enough for two, said, "Thanks," and pushed back his chair.

"Tapioca-and-prune dessert coming up," said

the foreman. "Wouldn't you care to wait and take a chanst on that?"

"I believe not, thank you kindly," said Rush. "Though I greatly admire it."

He went to the hitching post before the house, untied his bay and the mule, and headed north, out onto the plain. About a mile and a half out, behind a chain of wind-stunted bushes, he put the mule and mare on long pickets to graze for the night and unrolled his blanket. His stomach felt bladder tight from the meal and like paradise. He wondered if Spencer Eakins not only extra-fed his men but extra-paid them. Rush felt certain he did.

When he awoke in the early dawn there was a low prairie mist like a milky vapor over the grass. The sun came up and he put on his boots and shaved from his reserve canteen. With the sun, the mist turned to an instant of diamonds and burnt off.

The ranchyard was astir and the cook was bringing empty breakfast dishes from the house when Rush tied up again at the post and dismounted. Spencer Eakins lounged out onto the porch sleepily, a quill toothpick in the corner of his mouth. He saw Rush, remembered him, and said, "Morning. Everybody treating you right?"

"Mighty fine. As I'll sure tell Hayes and Mr. Hankinson."

"I'd appreciate it if you would," said Eakins. "By the way. You said last night you was fleein' from three fellers."

"Did I? I don't recall."

"Who was they?"

"I never heard their names."

"Would you care to describe them? Maybe I know 'em."

Rush considered. "They looked exactly alike, like identical triplets. They dressed city-style in fancy broadcloth and velvet and such and were very high fashion in their manners and the way they talked. They wore perfume." It wasn't a hard story to tell; all you had to do was say the opposite of everything.

"*Perfume?* You must mean barbershop hair tonic."

"I know the difference between hair tonic and perfume," said Rush patiently. "If I didn't I'd shoot myself."

"These are sure strange fellers," said Eakins. "I'll tell you one thing, I'll know 'em when I see 'em. You know what?"

"What?"

"I had three men that worked for me. Mr. Hankinson sent them down to Pelburg or some-place to do some work for him. They never came back. I thought in my sleep last night it might have been them. But it certainly ain't. I'd guess offhand it was some important city gamblers you had your ruckus with. What was this ruckus, by the way?"

"Them things are always hard to pin down. They just seem to get started."

"Did you steal something from them?" There was no reproof whatever in Eakins's voice.

"If you want the truth, they stole something from me. The life of a good friend."

"And they got you marked down as next, is that it? I've got to get you out of here, for Mr. Hankinson's sake. High-toned big city gamblers is more vicious than rattlesnakes and won't never give up. After you've had your breakfast you better set out, and I mean right now, for the old lumberin' camp. I'll tell you about it." He told Rush about it, its history, and the safest and quickest way to get there. It was about thirty-five miles away, to the northwest.

Concluding, Eakins added, "And if there happens to be anyone else there, it won't be more than a man or two, and they'll just be there to keep themselves out of sight for the time bein', like you'll be. They won't give you no trouble. Just tell them what happened to the major's mare and you'll all be blood brothers at the drop of a hat, using each other's tobacco and such."

Rush heard, but just barely. The one thing he had mainly heard was that it was Hankinson who had sent the three killers to Rann Clark.

"And by the way," said Eakins. "Jest what *did* happen to the major's mare?"

"It foaled," said Rush absently.

"It come over me that I hadn't really checked on you," explained Eakins, now satisfied. "I guess that's all."

Rush left him and started for the cook house. Last night, a stranger to the men, he had refrained from asking them any questions. This morning, they would be familiar with him, and be drowsy with sleep besides. This morning he had plenty to ask them.

In the open cook house door, he stopped and blinked. The men at the table were different men. This was a different crew entirely, even to the foreman at the far end of the table. This man was not blocky and oversized as last night's man had been, but scrawny and only about half as tall.

Hard, unfriendly eyes looked into his.

The scrawny little foreman said, "Who are you and what do you want?"

"I come from Jennington with a message for Mr. Eakins," said Rush. "Where could a man find him?"

"He should be in his house eating his breakfast about now," said the foreman.

Rush nodded and left.

When he left the ranchyard on his bay, the mule behind him, he headed not northwest as Spencer Eakins had previously directed, but dead east toward the rising sun, retracing the direction that had brought him in. There were cattle about him now, fat looking but travel-worn. When he came to the grassbowl, he saw that it was empty.

He was positive what had happened. The cattle enclosed in it last evening had been moved away in the night by the crew with whom he had eaten supper and were on their way to someplace else, who knew where. For that matter, who knew where they had come from originally? These travel-worn cows around him had been brought in by the men he had just seen eating breakfast. Spencer Eakins's ranch was a sort of relay station and probably collection point for the Hankinson ring.

Hankinson himself would have to wait, Rush decided; as he had said, he could always be found in Jennington. The important thing first was to know more about this thing, and how a fine man like Rann Clark could allow himself to be dragged into it.

Rush turned mare and pack mule northwest.

V

IT WAS about ten o'clock the next morning when he came to the abandoned lumbering camp.

He realized that since he had left Lister and Hayes's saloon he had actually described a big half circle, and must once again be not too far from the Musselshell.

All day yesterday it had been grassy plain, with sometimes a nuggetlike butte or two tiny on the horizon, until a few hours before sunset when the timber had started. By evening, he knew he was in it for sure and camped for the night by a spring, washed, shaved, and ate. Next morning, as he passed on, the virgin forest about him was as nice timber as he ever laid eyes on, tall, straight, uniform, level-floored, branches high in their canopy. Here and there, he pushed through saddle-high clumps of deep fern. After a bit, the ground began to be cut over, but not much. For awhile this had puzzled him, why it had been started then stopped. Then he realized it must have been the transportation part of it. You could have the best timber in the world but if it cost too much to get it out you'd better leave it strictly alone. There was a delicate balance there; exorbitant transportation could mean disastrous loss. Some-one had had a pipedream, and saw it wasn't

58

working out, and had been forced to give it up.

The light in the forest had been a hazy green from the tangle of branches overhead and then before him, through the tree trunks, he saw dazzling golden sunlight, and came out into the clearing of the camp itself.

The clearing was a natural oval, a hundred yards long and about half that across, ringed with sky-high trees, blazing golden in the sun, with a perimeter of makeshift buildings. There had never been trees within the oval, but brush, which had been grubbed out. Two log roads showed like gaps in the ring of trees, one leading back into the timber, and one leading down to the river, probably.

The buildings, Rush decided, were a work and repair shed, a roof open on all sides and supported by four corner posts; a low longish building, a stable for the logging teams, likely; and an L-shaped building which must have been sleeping and eating quarters. These were the most notable structures, but there was a miscellany of sheds also. None of the structures had ever been painted and neglect, plus maybe fetid humidity from the nearby river, made everything look a hundred and ten years old. Wild bean and bindweed vines grew everywhere there was anything upright, in big nestlike tangles.

There was no one in sight, but the place was used in a way, more or less, because there was a barely discernible trail through the oval length-wise, from the mouth of the road to the river to the mouth of the road into the forest. The part of the trail that led to the river, he was pretty sure, would tie in at right angles with a riverpath. These days about every river had its riverpath, or trail, winding along its shore, sometimes through two or three states, a rough trail generally, but one you could depend on.

He looked at the clearing and its buildings, first in an overall survey, then again in an item by item inspection. He was sure no one was here or had been here for some time.

Just about anybody who came here, he was certain after his talk with Eakins, he would like to talk to, and there would be someone here eventually, but how long would eventually be? He wanted this thing over quickly and how long a wait would pay him in the long run?

A long wait, if necessary, he decided.

Long wait, short wait, there were preparations to be made and he started to make them.

He went back a short distance into the forest with his mount and mule behind some sumac, picketed them, took the tarp with the heaviest gear off the mule to make it easier, laid it in the grass, took his saddlebags from his mare and started his return to the clearing.

About halfway there he stopped at a rotted fallen log he'd passed. He peeled off part of the bark shell. The wood beneath was runneled with insect tracings. He tested it with his finger. It was really rotten, all right, dry and spongy. He kicked it carefully into big chunks: two stagbeetles and a mess of plump white grub worms tumbled out of it.

He picked up a couple of the largest chunks—he could always come back for more—and all the while careful of nearby rattlers, and carried the chunks and saddlebags along with him.

Again in the clearing, he went directly to the stubby L-shaped building which had been the crew's quarters. Here, on a wooden peg outside the door, he hung his saddlebags and went inside with the wood, which he called *punk* but which his father's generation had called *spunk*. One side of the room was lined with double-bunks; there was an old cannonball heating stove with a rusty stovepipe guyed with wire to a ceilinghole, and that was all. They had taken everything with them when they left but the stove and he wondered why they hadn't taken that. He examined it, and soon saw why. It was useless. In its curved upper surface was a crack as big as his thumb.

He laid the punk on the floor before it and went outside. After a little searching, he found some clay behind the cabin. He took a double handful of clay inside and chinked up the crack in the stove.

This, he was sure, would hold and draw for

enough fire he was going to build in it. He put in the chunks of rotted log, lighted one corner with a match, and blew it into a little glowing rosebud of ember.

He then walked outside, stood a short distance away, and gave it time.

Soon the picture was just the way he wanted it, the saddlebags by the door, the little curl of smoke rising from the tin chimney-pipe.

There's a place that's occupied, he said to himself, smiling. *Anybody can see that.*

Of course, no horse dung around anywhere, or bent or broken weeds at its threshold, but any visitor here would probably have other things on his mind and not be too particularly scrutinizing. Any visitor here, according to Spencer Eakins, would likely be a man on the run.

And if Rush had such a caller, he wanted a look at him in advance. A man on the run, surprised, could be mighty nervous.

Across the clearing were two small shedlike buildings. Either seemed a good vantage point.

He went to the buildings.

The first proved to be a privy. *Whew!* Even safety wasn't worth a long wait there.

He opened the door of the second shed. It was small and bare except for a short shelf. On the shelf was food, about the sort you would find in a linecamp; cornmeal, a few cans of tomatoes, a rat-chewed flitch of bacon, two canisters, one with matches, one with tobacco and papers. Mr. Hankinson was thoughtful of his men, even his birds on the wing. There was a nice big knothole in the door. It was a perfect place, a perfect location.

He had just stepped out into the open again, for a last look around to be sure everything was as he wanted it, when he saw the man across the clearing, back to him, going through his saddlebags.

"I can't seem to find your tobaccy," said the man instantly, unalarmed, without turning, before Rush could speak. "Where do you keep it?"

Now he turned. He had a flat face and crinkled merry eyes. He wore a green plush cap with a black cardboard visor, a cast-off woman's coat with frogs and buttons up the left—the wrong side—ragged trousers, and dilapidated moccasins. Moccasins, not boots; he was a walker, not a horseman. He was a real woods tramp and a hell of a way from being as pitiful and merry and helpless as he seemed. A cougar could take care of itself; he could take care of himself. Under that buttoned coat, Rush knew, was a straightedge razor that had cut more than whiskers and could come out like magic.

Rush said, "You always go through a man's belongings when the man is out of sight?"

"Can you tell me a better time?" said the tramp, grinning. "What're you doin' here?"

"Homesteading," said Rush, poker-faced.

"Looks like you've picked a good place," said the man, joining in on the joke. "Good fertile ground. Might take a little clearing, though. Now that you've caught me, I'll be perlite about it. Could I borry some tobaccy?"

With his thumb, Rush gestured to the building behind him. "You'll find all the tobacco you want in there, and food, too. Help yourself."

The man vanished inside, was gone a moment, and came out drawing on a very fat brown paper cigarette.

He said, "The rest of the stuff, I left. The food I didn't touch. As a matter of fact, I'd choose catfish to rat-ate bacon." He puffed slowly, deeply, in delirious contentment. "You know somethin'? Over the years, I've used what willpower I've got and managed finally to shed off most human weaknesses. They's one, though, I can't seem to get rid of. Beholden."

"Beholden?" said Rush, actually becoming interested in this man.

"Yep, beholden. It's wormwood and gall to me to be beholden to anybody. They does me a favor, I gotta do them one right back."

Rush listened attentively; this, he realized now, was a deep character.

The man said, "I was tobaccy hungry. I consider this cigarette, instead of a bullet in the back as it could have been when you caught me, a special favor. I'm goin' to tell you something which may or may not be a favor in return. Last night, I made my camp in some scrub by the riverpath, back yonder." He pointed. "I was woke just after sunup by about nine horsemen coming up the path from the direction of the Spencer Eakins place. Eakins himself was in the crowd. They wasn't ridin' fast, but they was ridin' steady, and they wasn't jest out for an airin'—I seen parties like that before. They had to be headed for this place. This place was my next stop, too, so I took the shortcut. Through the forest. I'm a man that chooses forest anyways. Besides, I have to admit I was curious. Is that a favor?"

"Yes," said Rush.

"They should be due about now," said the man. "So you better dust unless you want to talk to them."

"I've already talked to them," said Rush.

"So I figgered," said the man. "Well, I ain't, and don't want to. Goodbye."

The forest swallowed him.

Rush watched him disappear. No one knew what he carried under that fabulous coat of his, maybe a short-barreled rifle he didn't want anyone to see and recognize, like, say, its owner, maybe even a half dressed rabbit he was saving for his lunch.

One instant he was by Rush, the next, hardly with movement, he was at the clearing's edge by the undergrowth, and then there was simply undergrowth.

The sound of horsemen came from the riverpath, still out of sight but picking up speed as they came.

He hit for the brush himself, fast. One thing he didn't want right now was a showdown with unimportant people, a mess of them, before he had his answer.

At the rim of the clearing nearest his horse and mule was a dense tier of pignut saplings with their big, waxy, hickory leaves. He made it, crawled into it, and rolled over on his stomach.

Nine mounted men rode into the clearing at a gallop, and, at a signal from their leader, slewed their horses to a scuffing halt in a dusty cluster around him. Their leader was Spencer Eakins and the man beside his knee was, of all people, Hayes, the barman from Lister. The woods tramp had been right. All told there were enough, and more than enough. They dismounted, took their rifles from saddle scabbards, and, at hand gestures from Eakins, threw a big loose circle around the building showing the chimney smoke and saddlebags.

Rush crawled backward through the foliage and made for his bay.

Behind him came shouts, and halloos, and yells.

If you want a good, noisy, safe time, thought

66

Rush, *there's nothing to equal shooting at an empty building.*

When he reached his animals, he saddled his bay, took in and coiled the picket ropes, deliberately and carefully, as he always did everything, lashed the tarp and the gear to the mule, and set out for Jennington.

Behind him, like a gray veil over where the clearing was, hung a pall of murky smoke iridescent with shimmering flakes of fire, gold and scarlet.

They were burning everything to flush him out, all the buildings, everything.

Hayes must have panicked, pocketed the eight or nine hundred dollars, passed up the garfish hole idea, and rushed to Eakins after all. With the true story. To save his neck. Naming himself an innocent witness.

And stirring up a hornets' nest.

VI

WHEN RUSH first encountered it, it looked like he would have to get rid of his pack mule. He didn't want to, for he had no idea just what his journey was going to be. Otherwise, however, the odds could be outlandishly against him. Eakins could send out messengers, hot with warning, and the sorriest saddle horse could make a fool of a man with a pack mule. Or maybe Eakins wouldn't, and Rush was inclined to favor this latter. He had a feeling that Eakins, having blundered, would try to keep it quiet and not advertise it.

Rush decided to retain the mule.

The fireball of the sun was deep in its western arc the following day, splintering itself across the roof ridges of the town, when Rush came again into Jennington. The glassy sky was high and cloudless and the rays of the red sun pinkened the dust motes of Main Street in a suffocating oven-like heat. He left the bay and the mule at a livery stable, figuring they each deserved a little luxurious food and grooming, extracted a promise of the same from the stableboy, tipped him decently to ensure it, and headed for Hankinson's office. The walk was deserted because of the sunset hour. Inside the batwing swinging doors of the saloon, he knew, many a tinhorn, just arisen, was having his breakfast of raw egg and tabasco washed down with half a tumbler of rye.

The office, when he came to it, narrow fronting, window painted green part way up, the green topped with a broad stripe of gold leaf, still showed the name: Thos. L. Grayville. Its door was wide open, propped so by a brass cuspidor used as a doorstop. Without altering his stride, Rush swung in. A man came forward from behind a desk at the rear, and met him in the center of the room.

The man was not Hankinson, but a new one to Rush, and he looked him over. He was young, with spectacles, with ink-stained fingers, and the ready-tied knot of his cravat was askew under the front of his giraffe-necked stiff collar.

The young man said, "Do I know you?"

"I was about to ask you the same question," said Rush, evading.

"I'm Mr. Hankinson's assistant."

"You're assistant to Mr. Hankinson, and Mr. Hankinson is assistant to Mr. Grayville," said Rush, knowing there was no Mr. Grayville.

"Just so," said the young man.

"Do you have an assistant?" asked Rush, beginning to enjoy the conversation.

"Of sorts."

"You can keep this up as long as I can, can't you?" said Rush.

"Yes," said the young man patiently. "It's one

69

of the things I get paid for. What brings you in?"

"I want to have a word with Mr. Thomas L. Grayville."

"He's in Boston."

"Then I'll send him a telegram. What's his address?"

"He has pneumonia."

"We're at it again, hey?"

"It seems so. And we always have eternity, don't we? Would you care to try a different approach?"

"Maybe I'd better. I'm Jim Pryor. Mr. Hankinson knows me. Where can I find him? No, I withdraw that. First this, the major's mare has foaled."

"What major?" asked the young man.

"Oh, no you don't," said Rush. "Not again. Not with me."

"Now if the major had foaled," said the young man, "or the major's foal had mared, that would be noteworthy. But I hear that other story several times a week."

"I'm whipped," said Rush.

"You'll find Mr. Hankinson in the back room of the Checker Front Saloon. I'm sorry you have to rush. I got a feeling, underneath, that I'm talking to a pretty smart cayuse. Come again. Will you shake hands?"

" 'Fraid to," said Rush. "You might well turn

out to be a topnotch wrestler, or a bowie-man, or something."

Neither of them smiled as he left.

The Checker Front Saloon proved to be one of those dens, even from its outside, that had given Rush a feeling of dislike on his previous visit. Without doubt, it was the worst place he had run into since he left Pelburg, he decided as he stepped inside. For one thing, it became too quiet as he entered. The room was not large and clean, and there were half a dozen men in it, rangemen from the way they were dressed, three standing at a short bar nursing or drinking beers, three in a corner at a circular ice cream table with twisted wire legs, playing seven-up. They had been talking, and they stopped talking. Rush had seen the same thing happen in certain poolrooms and barbershops. It was like the place was kind of a club and a nonmember had entered.

The bartender, florid and pig-eyed, called out hostilely, "They got better beer and whisky next door."

"That I can well believe," said Rush bleakly, slowing down. "But God knows I ain't here to quench my thirst or enjoy myself. I was sent here. I was told I'd find Mr. Hankinson in the back room."

"You will indeed," said the bartender, changing his manner, becoming almost fawning. "Just go through that door yonder, the one marked

PRIVATE." The customers went back to talking.

Rush crossed the barroom, stepped into the room marked PRIVATE, and closed the door behind him.

He had expected the typical back room, with maybe a small faro table for the elite and a few chairs. What he saw was a kind of storeroom, longish, with a row of barrels along one wall and a few cases of beer bottles along the other. Between them was a wide long space ending at the other end in a grimy fly-specked window. A few feet in front of the window, a man sat on a cane-bottomed kitchen chair, facing the door, his .44 out of its holster, resting on his kneecap.

The man sure as hell wasn't Hankinson.

He said in amazement, "Jim Pryor!" and got to his feet.

His voice was neither warm nor cold. He said it like you'd say, "That's a Sharps," or "That's a Winchester," or "That's a Henry," as an observation but an offhand matter of interest, too. He said it neutrally, yet at one time this man, Les Holburn, had crossed the Sierra Madres with Rush, alone, just the two of them, through the worst and hungriest of the high country, infested with the most savage of Yaqui and Apache, posses in front of them, posses behind them; they lived on just about anything they could get their fingerbones around and shared it equally, if not in friendship at least in hell-for-leather comradeship. It was the posse in front of them that had caught them. Rush had gone to Yuma, Holburn had gone to Huntsville. That had been in his professional gun-throwing days.

He said, "Howdy, Les. I see you're still at it. And never grew up. I was sent here for you, of course."

Holburn said nothing.

Rush said, "You in on this ring?"

"I'm in on no ring," said Holburn. "I'm strictly independent, always have been and always will be."

"But you're here to nail me."

"I'm here to nail whoever came through that door. That's the way it goes. You understand. You've done it yourself."

"Not this," said Rush. "Never."

So he *had* guessed wrong on Eakins. Eakins *had* rushed out the warning.

Rush said, "Did you have anything to do with Clark?"

"No. They weren't afraid of Clark. They're getting afraid of you."

"You wouldn't lie to me?"

"You know better than that."

"And why should they be afraid of *me?*" Rush asked.

"Jim Pryor is still remembered," said Holburn. "Hankinson knowed the name when you told him, he said, but just didn't let on. They know you're one of the best. They didn't think you was up to anything at first, but now they wonder."

"Was it Hankinson himself that paid you for this job?"

"Hankinson. Himself. Out of his pocketbook into mine. He's the number one man in the ring."

"I just came from his office," said Rush. "He wasn't there. I wonder where he is. . . ."

"That would be hard to say. This mix-up has got him spooked for the moment. He's somewheres, waiting for things to simmer down, I'd say. When I've finished here with you, I go around and report to the young feller that just sent you here to me, the one with the high starched gates-ajar collar—"

"I know who you mean," said Rush. "The talker."

"That's him."

There was a long moment of heavy tomb-like silence while they simply stood and stared at each other.

"You're fixing to kill me," said Rush.

"Money paid has to be earned."

Rush said, "If my ghost wanted to find Hankinson, say, and talk to him, where should it start looking?"

"That would be hard to pin down. Maybe Niles Station. Maybe it could ask around at the post office at Niles Station. Niles Station is a stop on the Pine Springs Shortline, which is a spur on the railroad about halfway between here and a town called Pelburg. You know what I'm going to do, Jim?"

"You just told me," said Rush expressionlessly, watching Holburn's gunhand like a hawk.

"The difference between a gunman and a gunfighter," said Holburn, "is that a gunfighter fights fair, even, and a gunman just gets his man dead and that's all. You're a gunfighter and I'm a gunfighter—"

"You were a gunfighter," said Rush. "You're a gunman now."

"I don't blame you for being spiteful," said Holburn seriously. "What I'm tryin' to say is that we're going to do this like honorable men. Fair and even. I'm going to holster my gun, I'm going to let you make the move, and I'm going to outdraw you."

Holstering his .44, he said, "I'll never forget those Sierra Madres, and the time you and me shared that lizard. Or how I cut that bullet out of your arm, or the look on your face when I made you finish the canteen, and you wouldn't touch it but pushed it right back at me."

Rush drew and shot. With no fuss and feathers, or tenseness, but just the utterly relaxed precision and accuracy which had once made him a reputation. "Like a second-card dealer," someone had once said of him. "He does it whilst you're watching, and nothing happens until it's all over."

75

Holburn fired too, and to a bystander it would have seemed he had fired simultaneously but there was already a bullet between his ribs, lodged in his heart.

Rush stepped over his body and headed for the window. He stepped over him without compunction, despising him, for he knew he was leaving a gunman on the floor, not a gunfighter.

In some last feeling of pride, perhaps, or craving for self-respect, Holburn had made his even-draw gesture. But the gunman streak had come through, the desire for the edge, the extra weight, the advantage, and he tried to throw Rush off balance by sentimental memories of their days together. Like reaching for the chalk when a pool player was on the verge of making a difficult stroke. But this was life and death. This was using old comradeship to kill a man.

Rush opened the window and stepped out into the alley.

When Rush walked into Hankinson's office, the young man with the ink-stained fingers and the gates-ajar collar was sitting at the desk, and Rush had to hand it to him: he didn't look terrified, if you didn't notice how his eyes seemed to pop open a little, just a little. With a steady hand, he finished what he was writing and came forward. He said, "A man named Holburn is looking for you."

"I've seen him," said Rush. "I just left him."

"Left him where?" asked the young man.

"On the floor," said Rush.

"Are you going to leave me on the floor?" asked the young man conversationally.

"Not me, not today," said Rush. "But I'd lay odds someone will, someday."

"What do you want with me?" asked the young man.

"Well," said Rush. "I'd like to borrow paper and envelopes and a couple of stamps for some letters, if you'd be so kind."

The young man laid the paraphernalia on the desk, said, "Help yourself," and walked to the front of the office, by the door.

Rush seated himself. Dipping pen in ink, he addressed an envelope to his wife, wrote on a sheet of paper, *Dearest Amy, hope you are okay, hope Joey is okay. Am okay myself. Love, Rush.*

He pulled a second sheet of paper before him, freshened his pen in the ink, and thought a moment.

Finally he wrote:

Dear Junior,

Here is the five dollars I owe you and which you have no doubt kissed goodbye to. If you should see Hankinson in that neck of the woods you might tell him the drove of pigs has long ago left Spencer

77

Eakins' place and is on their way, well on their way. Don't drink nothing I wouldn't drink though I do not know what that might be and stop using them loaded dice of yours in friendly games because that's when it comes quickest, I mean suicide, in friendly games.

> Your saddle pal,
> Orrie

He addressed an envelope to *Junior Adams, Niles Station Post Office. Niles Station, on the Pine Springs Shortline, General Delivery. Please Hold Until Called For,* enclosed the letter and a five dollar bill in it, sealed both letters, affixed stamps to them, and walked to the door.

"Where do I mail these?" he asked the young man.

"The depot is the best place," said the young man.

Rush mailed the letters. A little group of people, like a cluster of bees, was gathering before the door of the Checker Front. Rush got his mare and mule from the livery stable and left town.

VII

IF THE SHORTLINE was actually a spur from the main line, as Holburn had said, then the quickest and best way to find it was to follow the railroad tracks themselves until he came to the branch-off, and that was what Rush did. Railroad engineers knew their trade: the trackbed was level and for the most part straight—considering it flanked mountain foothills on his left—and he made good time.

Sometimes, as he rode along, his mind would go back to the Pelburg-Fort Justin road, in detail and in total, and wonder how the work in progress was coming along. Okay, he was sure of that. He'd observed John Sutton acting as straw boss many times, and there was a no-nonsense efficiency about him. He would remember Guffy, and grin to himself if he ever showed up on the work at all as he had promised, but which Rush doubted, Sutton would eat him alive.

He'd left Jennington Friday and late afternoon Tuesday he came to the switches and the fork in the rails, and turned right, along the spur, toward the mountains.

The grade rose. At first he was in a fan-shaped valley, and then he was in a climbing notch between piled-up wooded knobs, and finally in a gap, hedged on either side with sheer and tilted cliffs and bluffs of limestone, dazzling silver gray in the sunlight, pocked with great round holes like suspended caves, splintered with fissures sprouting wiry grass and leeched with vine runners. At times, it seemed to Rush, there was hardly enough space beyond the tie-ends for the clearance necessary for a train's passage.

Then, suddenly, the roadbed reached a sort of crest, and he came up out of the draw behind him into a plateau, as fine a stretch of grassy tableland as he'd ever seen. The tracks ran as straight as a ruler, diminishing ahead of him, across the turfy flat, which told him there must be a town of some kind past the skyline. There were a few cows in sight but nothing else.

Nothing else but the little building just beside him. A nice trim looking little two-room house with a big lettered plank over its door that said, NILES STATION, POST OFFICE. The door was open and a man in one-gallus overalls, barefoot, naked-chested, was sitting on the log doorstep, delousing a copper-colored chicken with a white powder, and giving himself a dash of it now and then behind the ears just for luck. When Rush rode up the man got up, grinned, and said, "Your horse don't show no sweat. That's a rough climb and your horse don't show no sweat. She must be a good mount."

"She is," said Rush agreeably, dismounting and

hitching. "My name's Junior Adams. You got any *Please Hold* mail for me?"

"Just come inside and we'll see," said the man.

Rush followed him through the door. The cabin's front room, walled with barked but unsquared logs, was a small supply and clothing store, with a few shelves of staples, and a few shirts and dresses hanging from the rafters. There was a short counter. The man stood behind it and said, "First off, I always give my visitors a little gift. What color do you want—red, green, or purple?"

"Well, I don't believe I want green, we can say that surely. Could I ask what we're talking about?"

"Candy jawbreakers," said the man taking a big square glass jar from beneath the counter. "How about red?"

"That'll be fine," said Rush, putting it in his pocket. "I'll eat it later. You had me scared for a minute there, from what I've been through. I was scared you were talking about whisky."

The man then produced a bundle of letters tied up with twine and leafed through them. "These is my general delivery," he said. "By gollies, here we are. Junior Adams." He passed the letter to Rush.

Rush took it and opened it. He extracted the five dollar bill, seemed surprised, put it in his wallet, and gave the letter itself back to the postmaster.

"When I was a boy," said Rush, "what with one thing and another, I never seemed to have time to learn to be a scholar. What in the hell does that thing say?"

The postmaster immediately began to put on airs. He donned a pair of spectacles slowly and with great dramatic effect, held the letter at arm's length from his nose, and said pompously, "Ain't no need to feel ashamed of it. Two-thirds of our deplorable population is in the same deplorable fix. Ready?"

"Yes."

"Git set!"

"I'm set. Let 'er rip."

The postmaster cleared his throat, and read the letter. He read it reasonably well, and with inflections, as though he were reciting Barbara Fritchie in a sixth grade English class.

"Thank you," said Rush. "I wish Orrie could have heard you. You sure made it sound exciting."

"You a friend of this Mr. Hankinson?" asked the postmaster.

"Nope," said Rush. "And my dice ain't loaded either. They just have certain inclinations."

"If you're not a friend of Mr. Hankinson, what you doin' carryin' him a message?"

"I ain't carrying him a message. I never heard of him," said Rush. "Orric has just got me mixed up with someone else."

"I'm a government man," said the postmaster. "On a government job with the mail and all, taking government pay. I ain't no friend of Mr. Hankinson, nor the opposite neither. Did you hear that? Nor the opposite neither."

"I heard you," said Rush.

"I live a lonesome life in a lonesome place," said the postmaster. "I like company, but not folks with a grudge agin me."

"And this Hankinson has a grudge against you?"

"No. And I don't want him to git one."

"That's understandable," said Rush obligingly.

"I'd appreciate it if you'd tell him so," said the postmaster.

"I wouldn't know him if I saw him," said Rush. "But I'll bear it in mind."

In the doorway, on the doorstep, the copper-colored chicken began to beat his wings, filling the sunlight with a nimbus of white louse powder. "If I took a change of mind and decided to pass along Orrie's word, how would I find him?"

"There you might have a little problem."

"How's that?"

"He only comes here every long once in a while. For a short rest. Or, you might say, as the vulgar puts it, to shake the fire out of his tail, to hide out."

"Is this a good place to hide out?"

"If you're kind to the Jowetts. Hankinson's mother was a Jowett."

"How do I locate one of these Jowetts?"

The postmaster pointed to the countertop. "Say

this is this-here high flatland we're on." He dipped his hand beneath the counter and came out with a fistful of yellow shelled corn and dropped it on the counter in a spraying motion. "That's Jowetts." Again, he put his hand beneath the counter and came up with a closed fist. "Red corn," he said.

He held his fist over the counter and opened it. It was empty. "The yellow kernels is Jowetts," he said. "The red kernels is non-Jowetts."

Rush said, "You mean Jowetts, and nothing but Jowetts?"

"Just about. Ever hear the expression 'degree of consanguinity'?"

"Yes," said Rush.

The postmaster ignored his answer. "It's mainly a court term nowadays, though the old-timers loved it, and my grandpa used to rattle it off free and easy even in breakfast talk. It means degree of bloodship. First cousins, second cousins, cousins once removed, twice removed, double, and so on. Well, this tableland is overflowin' with Jowett consanguinity. Different sizes, shapes, genders, faces, marriage names and such, but they stick together like glue."

"What kind of people are they?"

"Between you and me, very sorry. I hear they carry what they call Tennessee fightin'-knives. Barlows with all of the big blade cut off with a cold chisel but about an inch and a half. For cuttin' but not killin'. For fun and play strictly amongst themselves. Of course, they can accommodate a stranger otherwise, if the occasion arises, which it frequently does."

"I see," said Rush. "Thank you, and goodbye. I'm Jowett bound."

"Have a nice trip," said the man. "I wish I could sell you a return ticket, but I ain't God."

Five minutes later Rush was on his way again, headed away from the track at an angle, out onto the plain, the station behind him.

He had gone perhaps five miles when the grass began to thin and became blotched with patches of rock-dry yellow clay, and the flatland showed an edging of knolls in the near distance, backdropped by higher and yet more barren uplands. He was reaching, he knew, the back rim of the lush plateau. Cattle vanished, and gave way to nothing at first, and then a few goats could be seen, domestic goats but wild in eye and stringy tough and skeletal.

Around a thumb of cottonwoods he rode up suddenly face to face with two men digging a hole. They weren't dressed like stockmen, but more like dirt-poor hardscrabble farmers. They were obviously father and son: both were ferret-faced with shaggy black hair and wore cheap felt black hats, sweat-wet, which they wore even while they dug. The young one, the son, seemed about fourteen years old. When they gaped up at his arrival, snuff dribbled down their chins.

"Good day to you, gentlemen," said Rush in his most courteous manner, for he knew instinctively that good manners to these people would have been learned at the end of a parental horsewhip. "My name is Rush Ledderman. I'm from Pelburg, east of here. Stratton County." He knew that counties would be as important to them as family bloodlines.

"I never heard of no Pelburg," said the boy suspiciously.

"I have," said the father. "That'll be enough out of you, son. I'm Mayhew Jowett, and this is my boy, Mayhew Jowett."

"Glad to make your acquaintance," said Rush.

"Glad to make your acquaintance," mumbled the boy, relaxing a little.

"Glad to make your acquaintance," said the father. "All right, boy."

"That's a fine looking hole you're digging," said Rush. "What do you aim to put in it?"

"Nothing," said Mr. Jowett.

"Nothing?" said Rush.

"When we git finished," said the boy, "it'll put itself in it."

"Then that should save you trouble," said Rush, agreeable, but completely mystified.

"What the boy means," explained the father, "is that we're digging a well. For the cabin."

"Cabin?" said Rush.

"It'll be standin' about where your big bay is standin'," said the father. "It'll be the boy's cabin. If he ever gits started on it."

"When do you expect to start it?" Rush asked the boy.

"Ever'body says soon," said the boy. "I'm gittin' married."

"Congratulations," said Rush. "You mean you've already proposed to the girl and she has accepted?"

"So I've been told," said the boy.

"The girl comes from a mighty good bunch of the fambly," explained Mr. Mayhew Jowett. "Even though they's still some folks that doesn't hold with first cousins getting wed."

"I didn't exactly marry the girl: I married her father," said the boy. "I married that twelve-gauge two-barrel of his'n."

"You know what I married, son?" said the father reminiscently. "I was took with marriage one night behind a barn by five mean brothers and a passel of butcher knives at a wonnerful dance. Five fiddlers. You married, Mr. Ledderman?"

Rush nodded.

"Bird gun or butcher knife?" asked Mr. Mayhew Jowett.

"Deep meditation and freedom of will," said Rush.

"Well, at least they didn't threaten me with *that,*" said the boy.

Rush said, "I want to tell you why I'm trespassing this way on your private property. I want bad to talk to a man named Hankinson, from Jennington, and I hoped you could help me locate him. I was told some folks around here was kin of his."

There was a moment of stony silence as father and son stared at him.

At last, Mr. Mayhew Jowett said, "In a way I recall the name, but in a way I don't. I'll tell you what I'll do. I'll take you to Uncle Wilcox. If anybody can help you, he can." To the boy, the father said, "Son, you better git back to the place and fix that pen. Too many shoats been gittin' out."

The boy was off like a shot.

He was being sent as a runner, Rush knew. At the first house, he'd spread the word, and runners would go out from there, and so on. It would be hard for an outsider to believe how swiftly the story could be carried.

"Let's go," said Mr. Mayhew Jowett, still polite, but a little frosty now.

Rush dismounted, took his mare by the bridle rein, and walked beside the other, afoot. This, too, was to be courteous.

They threaded their way into the foothills, and seemed to walk forever. Rush knew he wasn't being led in a circle, that Jowett was too smart for that, with a direction finding sun in the sky, but that the journey was sure as hell being delayed. There was practically no conversation between them.

Finally, on a thinly wooded ridge, Mr. Mayhew Jowett came to a halt, pointed into a hollow just beneath them, and said, "Yonder." Rush could see the top of a longish cabin, its shakes, roofing slabs, held down by big chunks of rock. Mr. Mayhew Jowett yelled, "It's us!"

They descended the hillside and circled the cabin to its front. There were no women in sight, and that, of course, was one of the reasons Mr. Mayhew Jowett had yelled, so the women could scamper. At a ranch house, an approaching stranger could see women sometimes, at the well or on the doorstep preparing cucumbers for pickles, maybe. But at a hill cabin, never. You never saw them, but you could bet your life they were somewhere, peeping out, seeing you.

There was a long makeshift porch across the front of the cabin, and a porch of any kind on a hill house, Rush knew, meant prestige. This could very well be the home of the king bee of the whole clan. Five males were seated on chairs, tilted back against the cabin logs, seemingly at ease. One of them was young Mayhew, who had not only arrived ahead of Rush and his papa, but had apparently brought a few of his kinsmen along with him. Tattered black hats, muddy, patched and over-patched loose clothes, stiff knobby brogans, cowhide shoes with the rough side of the hide outside, they looked almost exactly alike. Except for the smaller boy at one end of the line and the old, old man at the other.

Rush's companion, Mr. Mayhew Jowett, said, "Uncle Wilcox, this is the man my boy has no doubt spoke of by now. Mr. Rush Ledderman, a very nice feller from a place called Pelburg."

The patriarch said, "I'm Wilcox Jowett. Welcome to Montana."

Rush said, "Pelburg is *in* Montana, a few miles down the railroad line."

"Thank you kindly for the educational information, suh," said the oldster. "Nobody can know ever' town. I do most of my tradin' at Niles Station, where they have them choice jawbreakers. These here are my boys, Wilcox, Whit, and Palmer, the originals. Chaffee couldn't make it."

"What do you mean, originals?" asked Rush, interested.

"Wal, nacherly, they has got children and children's children, and so on. So just about ever'where you go you'll find a Palmer Jowett or a Wilcox Jowett or a Whit Jowett or a Mayhew Jowett. As it should be."

"Any Jowett Jowetts, or Wilcox Wilcoxes?" Rush asked.

They all looked at each other, and shook their heads.

"No," said the old man. "But you got a red-hot

idea there, and they's shore as hell goin' to be!"

"Mebbe I can help," said the boy at the end of the line.

"The way I hear it, you've already helped," said the one named Palmer.

"Tom Hankinson's ma was one of my favorite daughters," said the old man abruptly. "She went away and married a man named Hankinson with a half-growed son and caught some kind o' red festers all over her body and died. The Hankinson you're talking about was jest her stepson, which makes him my stepgrandson, and only scholars can say whether that is actual kin or not, but we've always treated him as kin, in memory of his ma. He comes to us sometimes, without warning or notice, and departs without warning or notice. He ain't around here now, and it's been a long time since we've seen him."

"I wonder where I could locate him?" asked Rush.

"I wonder what you want with him?" countered the old man.

"That's between him and me," said Rush as graciously as he could.

"Then I'm afraid time is being wasted, yours as well as ours."

There was a glum, grim silence.

Suddenly, Rush felt that he was being horse-traded, and by experts. That he was like an

91

innocent colt being led in circles with a rope halter inside a corral.

He said, "I've asked you a simple question, you refused to answer it, and the way I figure it, that makes us even. You've got no cause to hold anything against me and I've got no cause to hold anything against you. I met Mr. Mayhew Jowett and his boy digging their well as a friend and I'd like to leave all of you as a friend. Therefore, with your kind permission, I'll ride on."

He sensed they weren't through with him, and hoped to bring the issue out into the open.

The old man, the patriarch, said, "If Tom Hankinson ain't at Jennington, or here, he's sure to be found at the Carlson road ranch. That's a place on the railroad, nigh it, about sixty miles east, I hear, of where the shortline spur join the main line. This road ranch, they tell me, ain't a depot or nothing, like Niles Station, but a trail stopover for the old time stockman before the railroad came. It's a hidey-hole fer him, jest as we're beginnin' to feel that's the way he considers us. You'll know him when you see him by a scar he got on each cheek when he caught a Cheyenne bullet."

Rush said, "I know him by sight. I've already met him. Once."

"You've met him and you want to meet him again. There's likely others feel the same way," said the old man. He didn't seem so fragile now; he seemed made of iron. "Can I tell you a little story about my boyhood?"

"I'd like to hear it," said Rush.

"I was borned and raised in the mountains in East Tennessee. We didn't have any near neighbors, and we was pore, and I had to make up my own fun, all alone. I found a little baby animal, alone like me and starvin', and brought it home and suckled it by hand on warm goat's milk. It would play with me and I would play with it and it would roll over on its back and pertend to play beanbag with me and all and in two months it had slew two kittens, a puppy coondog, and blood poisoned my thumb."

"What was it?" asked Palmer.

"A little bear," said Old Wilcox.

"Little bears is harmless," said Palmer.

"*Some* little bears is harmless," said the old man. "This 'un must have had rancid blood or something. It was an abomination to Babylon. Like Tom Hankinson."

"Like Tom Hankinson?" asked Palmer.

"We put up with him a long time," said the old man. "But he's finally bringing big-time killers into our country, and I got men, women, and babies to think of. When one comes, there'll be more to foller, and things'll change. Yo're a big-time killer, ain't you, Mr. Ledderman?"

"I'm a road builder," said Rush.

"Who told you to come here in the first place?" asked the old man.

"A man named Holburn," said Rush.

"Another road builder?"

"A big-time gun-thrower," said Rush.

"I see," said the old man, smiling faintly. "When you see Tom and get your own personal business over with him, I'd appreciate it if you'd tell him a few words from me. Tell him the Jowetts don't want to see him in these parts no more, never, and for him to forget those six .50-.90 Sharps Special cartridges I loaned him that time we was out hunting. We're all around quits."

"You know something, Mr. Jowett," said Rush. "I think you're a pretty good grandfather. You show mighty good sense, and take mighty good care of your flock."

"I try to," said the old man quietly. "But it shore adds years to your age; I'm only eighty-two. Mayhew, you brought him, you take him away. This time as far as Niles Station." To Rush, he said, "I don't mean to be unmannerly, but don't come back."

"I won't," said Rush.

As he turned his mount's neck by her rein, not quite wanting to leave on that note, Rush said, "But I am a road builder, as I said. And I do live just the other side of Pelburg. And I am married, like I told your nephew Mayhew. If you're ever over that way, we'd be pleased to have you drop in and have dinner with us." *That ought to do it,* he thought.

The old man bobbed his head formally. "Thank you for your invitation," he said in a noncommittal voice. "But what with taking care of my flock, like you call 'em, I'm a right busy man as you jest saw, and don't seem scarcely to get off this porch much of late."

VIII

A LITTLE SHORT of two days later, just in time for noonday dinner, he rode into the front yard of Carlson's road ranch.

There was a time he might have slewed up in front of it, fetlocks flying, and at first glance called a place like this home, but now, with his new life and all, he didn't much like the looks of it.

Three blocky little midget log cabins were crammed up into each other, with a squat common chimney of limestone rising up out of the meeting of their roofs. One of the side cabins, Rush knew, would have originally been a sort of dormitory, with built-in bunks, probably; the cabin at the rear would have been originally kitchen and the living quarters for the owner; the third cabin, the other side cabin, the one with the door, would have been the dining room and a kind of guest parlor.

Just as old Mr. Wilcox Jowett had said, it was about two hundred yards from the railroad tracks. Mr. Wilcox Jowett had said that this had been a stockman's rest; Rush could well imagine this having once been a cattle trail, and before that a war trail for Canadian Indians out of the far north, and before that, certainly, a buffalo

96

path. The railroad had changed

must come past steaming and pu.

throttle, with an engineer's wave, .

stop, for the grass between Carlso

the tie-ends was completely undistu

was a trail-like path past Carlson's

and this was being used, a little.

It was by this path that Rush approa
dismounted and hitched at the front door.

It might have been a road ranch on
quite possibly was a part-time road rancl
but mainly, Rush decided, it was a dw
for whoever might be its present occupan
occupants. For though it had pretty obviou
fallen into disrepair at one time, it had be
painstakingly rejuvenated, repainted—a brigl
orange—reroofed with cedar shingles, and decorated with windowboxes. In its front yard was a
garden plot of coxcomb and burning-bush plants,
neat but stomach-turning red, in the shape of a
star.

Somehow it put the hairs on the nape of
Rush's neck a-bristle in warning. It was clean,
all right, but a long time ago Rush had learned
that business about cleanliness being next to
Godliness could be wrong. He remembered a
little mountain inn run by a baby-faced German
and his *frau*. The bedsheets were stiff and white
and scented with lavender, the floors were so
scrubbed you could eat off them, and wouldn't

minded to, the food was so good. But many

st, rumor said, vanished in the night and it

a fact this German had the fattest hogs Rush

ever seen.

he fact that the road ranch looked so clean

neat, so extra clean and so extra neat, twisted

lf around in Rush's mind and made it look

ngerous to him. He knocked, so he wouldn't

rtle anyone into anything, and then, though

got no answer, and because a road ranch was

fter all a public place, he entered.

The room inside was a dining room, all right, and being at the moment used as such, which told him instantly, and without doubt, that the place was still being used—if only occasionally and part time—as a road ranch. If the structure were simply the dwelling of a small rancher, or farmer, the occupants, would be strictly kitchen-eaters. First, automatically, Rush glanced around for doors: one into the adjoining cabin, the original dormitory, at the left, and another to the rear cabin of the trio, the kitchen, at the rear. The doors were closed and everything seemed serene and secure. The floor was puncheon and had been lye-mopped for cleanliness until it was bleached. The walls were snowy white with lime, not only as an ornament but to act as a fumigant against crawling and flying things from outside.

The old road ranch table was still being used, a long trestle thing, but only the lower end was

in action, as you might say, the upper two-thirds being bare. Two men sat down at the lower end, the kitchen end, and a third, a gaunt, cadaverous-faced man with a square of wagon sheet belted around his waist as an apron, was placing a steaming tureen between the others, who sat facing each other.

One of them, with a florid, sun-peeling face, wearing homesteader's clothes and droopy slovenly boots, homemade, looked like a local farmer who had happened to drop in at noontime for a chat with his friend, the owner, and that was how Rush placed him. The other, small, thin, all tendons and white leather, would have impressed you as a run-of-the-mill cowhand, if he hadn't been wearing a gun as big as he was. It didn't look natural, seeing him spooning up that stew into his mouth, and seeing that gunbutt as big as a plowhandle jutting up beside him. He was dusty, too, with a yellow dust in creases and layers, in the notches between his fingers and such, and in patches across his forehead. He'd ridden hard and fast and far.

They were all strangers to Rush.

As Rush entered, the dusty man was saying, "He ain't in Jowett country back beyond Niles. They ain't seen him, and they don't want to see him. And this Jim Pryor had just been there, came and went. I've really got to find him now. Things is worse than he thought."

"Well, he ain't here," said the man in the apron.

"I think I'll have another helping o' that stew," said the farmer, ladling it onto his plate, ignoring them.

"I was told he'd be here," said the dusty man. "The Jowetts said he might."

"Well, he ain't," said the host.

"And more cornbread," said the farmer. "What are them little black things in it? Bugs or cracklin's?"

"Cracklings," said the host.

"Well, whatever they are," said the farmer, "I shore relish them."

"How about me?" said Rush, thinking he'd better soon join in. "Is there enough of that grub left for a hungry traveling-man?"

Six eyes, the farmer's beaming, the others stark, met his.

"I knocked," said Rush.

"I heard you," said the host. "But you didn't hear me say come in."

Then, from this, Rush knew the dusty cowboy had just arrived, and the conversation he'd just heard had been an emergency, and had to be risked, to be taken care of immediately.

"I knocked and didn't get any answer," said Rush. "I thought you didn't hear me, so I just came on in."

"Is that a habit of yours?" asked the host. "Knockin', not hearing no answer, so goin' right on in? I'd say it was a good way to get hurt. What if my wife had been standin' in the middle of the floor, taking a tub bath, as naked as a jay?"

"Then me, for one," said the farmer jovially, "would have been long gone. I'm afeared o' ghosts and your wife has been deceased for five years."

"Keep out of this, Elisha," said the host.

"I don't mean to talk loose," said the farmer. "But it always comes over me, it seems, when I've jest ate a big meal. Good grub snaps my watch springs quicker'n brandy."

Rush said, "I came in because I was told this is a road ranch and a road ranch is a public place, the same as a saloon, or a barber shop, or a feed store. And if it suits your fancy, it's just as easy for me to turn around and walk right out again."

He'd found out what he had wanted to know. It seemed certain from the conversation he'd heard that Hankinson wasn't here.

He looked at the dusty cowboy, and studied him, and tried to figure him out in the picture.

It seemed logical to figure that he was racing to Hankinson with the critical news that Holburn had failed.

After a period of sharp hesitation, the man in the apron said, "Of course you're welcome here, of course anybody's welcome here. But this is a home. It ain't been rightly a road ranch for fifteen years. Sit down. Who told you it was a road ranch?"

"An old lady on crutches, out looking for her bellwether," said Rush, seating himself next to the farmer. To the man across from him, the dusty traveler, he said, "I didn't notice your mount when I came up."

"It's in the barn out back, cooling down," said Elisha, the farmer. "You should have seen it when it come up, lathered like a new bar o' shaving soap and blowing like an elm bark whistle. That horse had been *rid*."

"Elisha," cautioned the host. "You're trying my patience."

He slopped a big heap of stew in Rush's plate.

"Better save a little of that for Mr. Eakins," said the farmer.

Rush laid down his big tin spoon.

He said placidly, "Do we have a Mr. Eakins in our party? I don't observe him amongst the convention assembled."

"He's the gentleman who took the horses back to the stable," explained the farmer.

So many things happened so quick that Rush was never later able to put them together in a picture that satisfied him. The door from the kitchen opened, a voice, startled and confused, bawled, *"Jim Pryor!"* and the rim of the tabletop by Rush's left hand exploded into flying splinters from a heavy gunshot. He rolled to the floor under the table to protect himself, twisting, snapping his hammer once as he went. Later, he remembered seeing Spencer Eakins in the doorway ten feet away, revolver in hand and a bewildered sag to his jaw; behind him was a cooking stove and a ham hung from a meathook on a rafter. Eakins's jacket was open and there was the belt buckle, two-pronged and bigger than a turkey egg.

If you're in a terrible hurry, or your target isn't in the clear, wise old masters had instructed him when he was a youngster just going on the gun, *right above the belt buckle is the place; it'll bring 'em to the floor like they was axed, and ten to one it'll catch some bone inside and maybe slap up even into their heart; it's the way out, the safety shot, and don't you ever forget it.*

Then a gun snout and a dusty face poked down from above. The face, peering, was scarcely a handbreadth from his.

He blew it to pieces.

He climbed out and stood up and there were three men on their feet, himself, the host, and the farmer. Spencer Eakins proved to be dead. "The other one is dead, too," said Rush. "I wonder who he was."

"All I knew him as was Bucky," said the man in the apron. After a deep breath, he added, "I've got nothing to do with all this, and I want to tell you something, mister. In all my borned days I never saw a gun as fast as yours."

"If you'd been some of the places I've been," said Rush coldly, "and seen some of the men I've seen, you'd have seen faster." Then he asked, "Hankinson isn't here?"

"No, sir, he ain't," said the host.

"Where is he?"

"I don't know. If I did, I'm shore in the spirit to tell you. These fellers, Bucky and Mr. Spencer, didn't even know themselves. They was lookin' fer him. They thought he might be here, but he ain't been. Wherever he is, it's somewhere else."

Elisha the farmer, and the host, whose name turned out to be Amberson, and Rush buried them at the end of the barn, where the soil was loose and easy to spade up. There was a custom in such cases, not generally much discussed but frequently followed, of stripping the bodies, piling up the effects of the deceased, and dividing them among the survivors concerned. In this case, the custom was carefully avoided. Guns, wallets, clothes, boots, everything was carefully left in order and so interred. There would be repercussions here from Hankinson or his friends, Elisha and Amberson feared, and they wanted to be able to say, "Here they are. Exactly as we put them away after this Pryor killed them. Untouched. Nothing missing."

When they had finished the burials, and Amberson had meticulously cleaned the loam from the spadeblades with a corncob, like any good gardener, Elisha came up to Rush and said, "Friend, my cabin's only a hoot and a holler from here. Would you do me a favor? I'd hate to admit it in public, but I don't know a thing about firearms and I got a old flintlock pistol with a trigger that won't quite work. Would you take a look at it and maybe tell me how to fix it?"

"I'd like to," said Rush. "But I'm no expert on flintlocks, and besides, I'm in a rush. I might not know where I'm going, but I'm in a rush."

"You know gunlocks, don't you? A flintlock should be as easy as pie for you."

The farmer's florid face, hidden from the road ranch owner, screwed up in a gigantic significant wink.

"Git your horse," said Rush. "I'll meet you out front. When you come right down to it, it's a small return for what you just did for me."

Amberson went into the kitchen door. Elisha headed for the barn. Rush made his way to his bay and mule out front, unhitched and mounted.

Elisha rode up on a huge gray dapple, not a saddle horse, but a workhorse, and a splendid creature. He rode without saddle but with a fold of blue and white bed ticking over its back. "Let's go," he said.

They started off.

Elisha said, "You ever deal in horses?"

"No," said Rush. "I'm a road builder."

"I know. I just seen you a-buildin' roads. Move around quite a little, do you?"

"Of late, yes."

"Dealing in horses on the side, while you go, would be a mighty good way of picking up a little spare cash."

"I don't know 'em well enough to go into the business. A good professional horseflesh man could skin me out of my hide."

"Not if you bought 'em cheap enough."

"They don't come that cheap."

"They do if you know where to get them."

"And where would that be?"

"Well, let's say, for the heck of it, if you got them from me."

Rush was careful not to look at him; he said, "Do I know you well enough to ask *you* where you get them?"

"No offense meant, but no, you don't," said the farmer.

"From Hankinson or any of his pals?"

"No," said the farmer. "But I will say this: it was Amberson back there who put me onto the feller who put me onto the parties I deal with, and though Amberson is friendly with

106

Hankinson it has nothing at all to do with any part of Hankinson or his operation. This one is so small and independent that Hankinson wouldn't even fool with it. He knows about my parties, o' course—he knows about everything—but he leaves them be, and they leave him be."

The country was full of small-time horse thieves, Rush knew, working in little bands of two or three, and always ending up on a lonesome creek under a tree limb in a noose of rope.

"Not interested," said Rush.

It was just about then he had his shock.

He heard the whinny of a horse, a whinny he was sure he knew, almost in his ear.

He glanced down at Elisha's mount, the huge dapple gray workhorse. It was gray, yes, but a little on the brindle side and that was why he hadn't noticed immediately. The faint brown brindle had thrown him off.

When he had last seen that horse, it had been pure gray. Since then it had been toughed over with sepia, artistically, not too much, just enough.

It belonged to John Sutton, his straw boss, and should be back on the Pelburg-Fort Justin road. There was the brand: *J-reversed-S.*

He said, "We'll go to your cabin and fix that flintlock."

"I don't have any flintlock," Elisha said. "I jest made that up to get to talk to you."

"Maybe we can fix it anyway," said Rush.

"That's what I like," said Elisha. "A man that thinks things over, and changes his mind, and decides to become reasonable and listen to a little more on the subject."

IX

ELISHA'S CABIN, when they came up to it, impressed Rush as any ordinary good-dirt farmer's cabin, a little better than average, maybe. He would have said from the general setup that Elisha was prosperous, but not downright opulent. Things, the cabin, the double barn and the corral behind it, the fences, the housing to the well, were cared for and in good repair which was the way, a lightning rod salesman had once told him, to calculate the occupant's bank account. A farmer careful about his yard, the salesman had said, would be careful about his fields and stock and equipment. A sorry yard meant a sorry farmer. It seemed like Elisha must be a pretty good one. Rush decided, too, that he must be either a widower or bachelor, for there were no curtains at the windows of the house, even cheap muslin, but only green roller-blinds, pulled halfway down.

Rush cut his eye at the man beside him as they rode.

Elisha was completely composed, untroubled, and seemed utterly unconcerned about anything at all. His blubbery body didn't seem so blubbery now but bunchy-muscled, and though he had a little potbelly that jiggled to his horse's pace up against his saddlehorn, his seat and posture were topnotch and Rush knew that he was seeing a man who was a number-one horseman.

From behind the house, a young male voice broke out in song.

"Sounds like I got visitors," said Elisha. "Let's go look at 'em."

They rode to the rear.

Two swarthy, tough-looking young men, in their early twenties, maybe, were sitting cross-legged on the packed earth near the kitchen door. They got to their feet as the newcomers rode up. One of the young men wore mustard yellow chaps, tight, legging style and the other was noticeable for his stiff leather cuffs, almost elbow-length, decorated in nailhead brads. Rush wouldn't have liked either one of them near any stray cash of his, lying, say, on a bartop.

"Howdy to you, gentlemen," said Elisha, appearing pleasantly surprised. "You got something to say to me?"

"Yes," said the man in the leather cuffs.

"What?"

"It can wait," said the man.

"Don't be afraid of my friend," said Elisha, jerking his thumb at Rush. "You can say a little, but no need for it to be too much, in front of him. He's all right."

"We brought you something again," said the man in the leather cuffs.

"Where are they?" asked Elisha.

"Same old place. At the crick fork," said the man. "You owe us each a hundred dollars."

Elisha asked, "How many?"

"Eight," said the man in the cuffs. The man in the yellow leggings just stood and listened. Elisha took out a giant roll of bank notes and paid each of them.

Stolen horses, of course, Rush knew. Eight for two hundred dollars: twenty-five dollars apiece. No wonder Elisha had said he could get them cheap. And they'd be at least medium good. The thieves wouldn't want to hurt their market. And a hundred dollars would mean many a day's honest work.

Now the man in the yellow leggings said, "A minute ago you said this friend o' yours was reliable. What makes you think he's reliable?"

"He's one of us, someway," said Elisha. "He has to be. I just saw him gun down two men at Amberson's, and one of the men with the first shot and behind him."

They looked impressed, even respectful.

The man in the yellow chaps said, "Who were these men he gunned?"

"Bucky Harris and Spencer Eakins," said the farmer.

"Spencer Eakins, I heard of," said the man. "But Bucky Harris, I never. Spencer Eakins is a Hankinson man from up at Lister."

"Bucky is too," said Elisha. "They come in together."

"Is that the way you spend your time?" the man asked Rush. "Going around killin' Hankinson men?"

Rush made no answer.

"What's your name?" asked the man. "And if you don't like the question, forget I asked you."

"James Ludlow Pryor," said Rush.

"Down on the Brazos they say Jim Pryor's in jail!"

"Down on the Brazos they claim house cats is mountain lions," said Rush.

"We want no part or parcel of no difficulty with Mr. Hankinson," said the man in the yellow chaps. "No, sirree!"

"Why not?" asked Rush.

"Well, for one thing, if worst came to worst, he'd put Holburn on you!"

They unhitched the mounts from a short rail, a couple of serviceable looking pintos and mounted. They reined their horses, rearing, to their hind legs, whirled them, spurring. The man in the leather cuffs bawled, "See you later, Elisha. Maybe yes, maybe no," and they were off over the grass, first at a gallop, then at a dead run.

"They'll be back," said Elisha, with the judicial air of a robed judge. "And they'll keep comin'. Until some rancher lays up in a ravine some night

with a Krag-Jorgensen five-shot bolt action .30,
and puts them out of business."

They stood there mutely while the backyard
dust settled.

Finally, Elisha said, "Well, how about it?"

"How about what?" asked Rush.

"You heard it," said the farmer. "I just bought
eight horses for two hundred dollars. I'll sell you
the whole string, here and now, for three hundred
dollars."

"Sight unseen?"

"I bought them sight unseen, didn't I?"

"You people sure have a funny way of horse
dealing," said Rush. "Mostly when a man buys
a horse, even a single horse, he almost makes a
marriage ceremony out of it, parading the horse
and watching it, inspecting its eyes and teeth, and
so on. Sight unseen!"

"Under these conditions, that's the best way,"
explained Elisha. "You can be mighty damn sure
of getting more than you're paying for. They
wouldn't sting me because they need me: I mean
quick safe money to them. And I wouldn't sting
you because you could really do me damage
with a sheriff. It's up to you, but I'd advise you
to take the gamble. There could be big profit
here."

"I don't know," said Rush, pretending to falter.
"A stole horse is hard to get rid of. Especially for
me. I'm new at it."

"No worry there. I'll fix that part of it up for you."

"How?"

"I'll give you a bill of sale. For each and every one of them."

"Anyone with a pencil and a piece of paper can write a bogus bill of sale. And in this country, these days, this is a fact well known. A bill of sale is no guarantee anymore to a suspicious buyer."

"Mine are," said Elisha.

Rush looked tantalizingly amused and skeptical. "In what way?"

"My bills of sale are notarized, with the notary's seal."

"Are you a notary?" asked Rush, surprised.

"No."

"Could I see one?" asked Rush.

"Sure," said Elisha. He went into the house and returned with a sheaf of papers which he handed to Rush.

They were all alike, bills of sale printed in the proper legal form. Printed, not scrawled with a pencil against the side of some barn. At the bottom of each bill, after the blank space which would contain a description of the article sold were two blanks, one for the seller, one for the buyer, and at the side of these two more blanks, for two witnesses.

At the bottom, in a corner was the notary's seal,

the seal of the state of Montana, and beside it the name of the notary who had placed it there and made the transaction official.

Harlowe Tate, the signature said, *Pelburg, County of Bratten, State of Montana.* There was a line for the date, also left blank.

Rush flinched.

A blank, but notarized, bill of sale was highly illegal. And mighty useful to stock thieves.

He knew that Tate was one of Pelburg's two notaries, along with the sheriff's wife, and it was a blow to him.

His old friend I-Buy-and-Sell-Anything Tate apparently did just that, including criminal ready-made bills of sale.

This was no proof, or even absolute indication, that he dealt in stolen stock itself. *Just with the stealers,* Rush thought dryly.

He handed the papers back to Elisha.

"This is getting too deep for me," he said. "I don't believe I'd better touch it at all." Then he said, "I'm going to ask again, Hankinson isn't in on this in any way?"

"In no way whatever," said Elisha.

"I believe it," said Rush. "But I just had to be positively sure before I left you."

Elisha said, "Then we can't negotiate, and this is all?"

"We can't negotiate," said Rush. "But this isn't all."

The farmer, his rosy face flaccid and relaxed, waited.

Rush said, "That big dapple you were riding, the one that was gray but has been touched up with brown. The one with the *J-reversed-S* brand. It was taken from a friend of mine, John Sutton."

"I wouldn't know," said Elisha, making no effort to deny it.

"How many others of his did they take?"

"No others, the way they told me. They just had a good chance at this one."

"Get it back."

"How?" asked Elisha.

"You'd know more about that than I would. Get it back."

"If you say so," said the farmer.

He stood in the blazing sun, face impassive, and watched Rush depart.

The rest of that day, and the next, and deep into the night of the third, he moved due east, retracing the direction from which he had come, with Pelburg as his destination.

Retracing the direction from which he had come was to be his journey, it seemed: Pelburg, Jennington, Lister, Lister, Jennington, Pelburg.

Part of his mission he left behind him, accomplished: his execution of Rann Clark's three assassins. But part, the major part, was still unfinished. He had to know how that honorable man, Rann Clark, had been dragged down into a world of criminals, who had done it, and what outlandish pressures had been exerted to bring this about. Pelburg and his old friend, Tate, he was sure now, held these answers. The conviction in his mind that this was so didn't sicken him, as he would have expected. It drove him into a black rage.

It was at the blackest pitch of the black moonless night, about a quarter after two, when Rush came into Pelburg. It didn't seem like his boyhood town now, it seemed simply like any point in the hundreds of miles he had just traveled, a path to Hankinson and maybe a few questions and answers, and the wretchedness from his mind gone forever. If Tate could tell him about Lister and the three gun-trash murderers, maybe Tate, with the levering bar he had against him, the bogus bills of sale, could remember and tell him something about Hankinson. He went down Main Street, brick and frame, past the square and jail and courthouse, to the alley by the Gem Saloon, and turned his animals into the alley.

When he came to the shack in its yard of rubbish and junk, he dismounted and hitched. The single window, with its sheet of newspaper pasted over the inside of the glass, showed lamplight. Rush took out his gun, held it loosely by his knee, and knocked, the old signal knock, three, three, one. He took out his gun in advance because, frankly, after his visit with Elisha, he didn't know what he might be getting into. The Tate he'd thought he'd known was not the Tate Elisha knew, that was sure.

The jolly, high-pitched voice called out from within, "It's a little late, but come in."

Rush stepped inside.

"Why, it's Rush," said Tate. "And carryin' somebody else's gun."

"Carrying my own gun," said Rush.

"Then why ain't it in its holster where it belongs?" said Tate, looking puzzled.

His bald head shone in the lampglow like waxed brown leather and his puny little body looked like a dead leaf after you'd crushed it in your hand. He not only looked harmless, he looked pitiful. He sat at his table mixing ingredients from little bottles marked prussiate of potash, prussiate of iron, and others, into a big water-filled wine bottle, making homemade ink. "Have a drink?" he asked, smiling.

"I drank worse up at Lister," said Rush. He didn't smile in response.

"And seen them three fellers while there. And properly medicated them, I figger."

"How do you figure that?"

"Because you're back. And hale and hearty. But there's more, too."

"What more?" asked Rush.

"You left my friend and come back my enemy.

Somehow, for the life of me I can't figger how, you've heard things and half things about me you didn't know before, and have twisted them around in your mind and come up with the idea that I, myself, might have had something to do with Rann Clark's murder."

"You said it, not me," declared Rush, stiff-faced, for it hadn't occurred to him.

"If so, you're wrong," said Tate, his little eyes looking very alert and very wise. "So put away that gun."

Rush ignored the suggestion. He said, "While I was gone, I saw you were flooding the north country with blank notarized bills of sale. That means, for one thing, that you're betraying your county, your state, and your country. A judge once told me when I was young and frolicky that if you even broke a village ordinance, it was same as treason against your country. For law was law, and there was no such thing as big laws and little laws."

"And you believe that?"

"I didn't then. But I do now. Since he set me down and explained it to me, I've got religion." Seriously, he asked, "What kind of a man are you, really?"

"Pretty worthless, I guess," said Tate. "According to you and your new religion. You're aimin' to six-gun me, ain't you, son? No matter what?"

"Don't call me son," said Rush. "And about

the other, all you've been doing is setting there talking out death warrants for yourself. Did you have any connection with Rann Clark?"

"Me and him and you was close friends, remember?"

"I mean monetary."

"None at all, in any way."

"Do you have any connection with Hankinson?"

"Same answer."

"If this last one was a lie," said Rush, "it was a good place to use one."

"Why, may I ask?"

"Because I found out for sure it was Hankinson who sent them three down here to kill Rann Clark. Did you and me ever discuss Hankinson before?"

"I don't think so."

"Well, you sure fall into the swing of it mighty easy."

"And now you're layin' traps with words," said Tate. "That's a low-down habit to get into, and I advise you stop it before it grows on you. It's sneaky, and you're a better man than that, Rush Ledderman."

Rush put his gun in its holster. "But you know Hankinson?"

"Not well enough to give him a cigar, and light it for him, and brush lint from his shoulder, but I know him on sight. You get to know all kinds of people in my business, some well enough to whisper into their ear, some just by sight."

When Rush spoke again, his voice was slightly friendly, not as friendly as it had been once, but not touch-and-go dangerous. He said, "You know something, Harlowe, I made a long trip to the well, and came back empty. You could say I only learned one thing."

Tate, with his little dried pea eyes, just sat and waited.

"What I learned was that there was a gap, an important gap, in what I knew about Rann Clark himself. I knew him before I went to jail the last time, and I knew him after, when I came out and he made a human out of me, standing behind me that way; but in between is the gap."

"In what way?" asked Tate.

Rush said, "I know what I was doing when I was in jail, but I realize now I don't know anything at all about what *he* was doing when I was in jail."

"What *could* he have been doin'?" asked Tate.

"Well, for one thing," said Rush, "that was the period he sold out and retired. I went away and he had a nice herd. I came back and he had no herd, and money in the bank, and nothing to do all day but school Joey and sit around and slap sweatflies or try to invent a new fish lure with snips of sardine cans."

"The lucky dog," said Tate enviously. "He's the only retired man that retired when he retired."

"What became of the cattle?" asked Rush. "Where did they go? Who did he sell them to?"

"They was bought by the Department of Indian Affairs. For the Bannock Reservation down at Fort Hall. There's nothing funny there. You can trace it easy, if you want to bother."

"I don't," said Rush.

"Well, he must of come up agin Hankinson some way, some way we don't know about," said Tate. "And crossed him. Or Hankinson wouldn't have had him killed."

Rush said dully, "It's not that he crossed him that worries me, it's maybe that he *double-crossed* him."

Shocked, Tate said, "An upright man like Rann Clark would never have no dealings with a cattle thief like Tom Hankinson!"

"I hope not, for my feelings toward him, as well as for Joey's sake," said Rush. "But who would ever have thought an upright man like Harlowe Tate would have dealings with Elisha, the horse thief?"

"I guess you'll hold that one agin me forever," said Tate. "Now that you're finally home, what do you aim to do?"

"That's hard to say."

"But anyway, we're friends again?"

Rush said nothing.

"They always told me silence gives consent," said Tate. "I'll take that to mean yes."

X

AMY AND JOEY were overjoyed when he rode up to the cottage. In the first phase of his return, from his arrival until after noonday dinner was finished, they were, each of them, careful not to question him. He bathed, twice in succession, in fact, first using Amy's homemade laundry soap and then her drugstore castille from the county seat, shaved, and put on stiff clean clothes from the skin out. After dinner, after the preserved cherry pie with its high meringue topping, they got to work on him, piecemeal and in rotation, and with persistence and repetition sucked the whole story out of him. He answered truthfully and in detail, only toning down his experience at Hayes's saloon at Lister and his gunfight with Holburn—for their sensibilities—and omitting the road ranch incident entirely. He didn't mention Tate's bogus bills of sale either.

"But you didn't find out why my father was killed?" asked Joey.

"No, Joey, I didn't," said Rush. This was the time to be honest with the boy.

He spent the afternoon inspecting a section of the road and saw that Sutton (with Guffy's meddlesome help, if Guffy *had* helped) had done a fine job. Everyone was quietly but efficiently busy. The new covering on the old bed was of the right depth, evenly spread, had the right grade, and the drainways along the berm were well shaped and properly continuous. The old culverts had been unclogged, according to the stipulations of the contract, and where new culverts had been added—mainly because of Guffy's complaint about the watershed—they were being well done. Rush got home about suppertime, washed his hands and face at the enamel basin on the back porch, sluiced the dirty water from the basin on the rosebush by the doorpost, as was the family custom—in the belief that soapy water kept down aphids—and went into the table. In those moments he could get Hankinson out of his mind, he felt pretty good.

When the meal was finished, Rush and Joey took four chairs out to the east side of the house, the cool side, one for each of them and Amy, and an extra one to look hospitable, and had a little talk while Amy did the dishes. Rush said casually, "Why don't you live with us? Why don't you let us adopt you?"

Joey held a kitchen match on his knee, broke it into halves, and the halves into halves. He said, "Was my father adopted?"

"No," said Rush.

"Were you?"

"No, to my sorrow."

"I'd like to live with you," said Joey. "But the

other part, I'd like to study a while. I may turn out to give you trouble. I may turn out to be a maniac or something."

"Then this would be just where you belong," said Rush. "Amy and I are both maniacs. Me more than Amy, but sometimes she leans that way."

Amy came out, nibbling a beef rib, and joined them.

"See?" said Rush. "Not four minutes ago she wolfed down a gluttonous supper and has forgotten it already!"

Seating herself, Amy said, "Don't pay any attention to him, Joey. He talks like a maniac half the time."

Joey's eyes bugged. He said doggedly, "I don't care. I love you both, anyway."

John Sutton drove up in a buckboard and got out, slowly and deliberately. Everything he did was deliberate, tediously deliberate. He was a rancher, all bone and stringy muscle and tendons, and as tan as walnut stain. He was a man you could depend on like forged iron if he chose to trust you and give part of himself, even a tiny particle, over to you. This was the man Rush had chosen to manage the project while he was away. He was known as a man of very few words, and Rush, unconsciously falling into his style, said simply, "Howdy," and pointed to the empty chair.

Sutton nodded, and sat down.

Amy said sociably, "What's been happening out at the Sutton place? How is Mrs. Sutton?"

Sutton balled the fingers of his right hand into a big fist about the size of a batch of biscuit dough, tightened it, and held it out for her to inspect.

"He means he hit her," said Joey, shocked.

Sutton shook his head.

"Maybe he means *she* hit him," said Amy.

Again Sutton shook his head, and pointed to his jaw.

Rush said, "He means she's got a toothache as big as his fist, the swelling is."

"And hollers all night," said Sutton, taking a flyer into words.

"Terrible," said Amy sympathetically. "Would you like some oil of cloves?"

"Not me, her," said Sutton.

"I mean to take back with you?"

"Be grateful," said Sutton, and sounded as though he meant it. This polite social prelude over, Sutton said, "I brought my report."

"You shouldn't have gone to all that trouble," said Rush. "But thank you. I'll look it over after you leave, just before I go to bed."

"Not wrote, spoke," said Sutton.

"Fine," said Rush, settling back. "Let's hear it."

"Okay," said Sutton.

Rush waited. Nothing more emerged.

Finally, Rush said, "You mean that's it. That's your report. Everything's okay?"

Sutton nodded.

"That's what I call a good report," said Rush. "Though I'd call it a little modest. I looked over about six miles when I got in, and it looked better than okay to me. It looked superfine."

"It was supposed to."

"See Mr. Guffy on the job?" asked Rush.

"Said you sent him," said Sutton, smiling very faintly.

"And you knew why?"

"I knew why."

"Did he bother you?"

"For three days."

"Then what?"

"Then I bothered him."

"How?"

"I told him what I thought of him."

"And he never came back?"

"I had a road to build."

"John," said Rush seriously, "in my recent ramblings and travelings, what did I run into but a big dapple gray that had been stained light brown, and with a *J-reversed-S* brand?"

Sutton sat stiff as a poker.

Rush said, "It's going to be returned. It'll show up sometime when you least expect it."

Sutton, suddenly becoming voluble, said, "I've got to know more about this, Rush. It was took from my pasture. And there hasn't been a day of my life I would rather have the thief than the horse."

"I know. I'm sorry. But that's the way it'll have to be. And John, I'm not finished. Could you keep on for a while?"

"Why, nacherly, Rush."

Sutton had gone, night had fallen, and they were inside, Amy and Joey lighting lamps and Rush at the kitchen table having a cup of coffee, when there was a knock at the kitchen door. Rush answered it. It was a man known in the community as Little Billy, one of Guffy's cowhands. He said, "Mr. Guffy sent me to welcome you back and collect that pack mule and save you a trip, if it's all right with you?"

Guffy certainly kept track of his property. Rush asked, "How much did he say I owed him?"

"That's what neighbors is for," said the man. "To do favors for other neighbors. Where will I find it?"

"Out back in the barn," said Rush.

Amy gave the man a piece of coconut pie, and he was gone.

Amy poured herself a cup of coffee and seated herself at the table by Rush's side. Joey joined them with his arithmetic. Amy said, "You know what I've been craving all day? A big chunk of chocolate cake topped about two inches deep with a mound of piccalilli relish."

Joey raised his eyes and gawked.

Rush said, "Made a little discovery while I was away, eh?"

"It was Dr. Alexander who actually made the discovery," she said.

"Blessed event?" said Rush softly.

"There seems no doubt about it."

Joey, who had been trying to follow the gist of the conversation, and who was completely befuddled, said, "Chocolate cake with piccalilli relish on it doesn't sound like a blessed event to me. But as my daddy used to say, tastes differ."

"When you've learned that lesson, you've got life whipped," said Rush.

He picked up Amy's hand, kissed it tenderly, and gently replaced it on the table.

"That was the reason, especially," said Amy, "that I was glad to see that man come a few minutes ago and get the pack mule and take it back to Mr. Guffy. Without the pack mule, you won't be traveling anymore. You'll be at home with us."

"I'm sorry, but no," said Rush. "I've got to go out again. And a man travels fastest without a pack mule."

"But why?" demanded Amy.

"I've got to talk to Hankinson. I've got to. I owe it to Joey."

"You've done your best and failed," said Amy. "It's no disgrace when a man has done his best."

"I didn't fail," said Rush. "I just stopped too soon. He's somewhere."

"You know what I think?" said Joey. "I think he just tucked himself into some hole and laughed at you while you passed him by."

"I'm getting that feeling myself," said Rush. "I'm going to make the whole circuit again if I have to, Pelburg, Jennington, Lister, Lister, Jennington, Pelburg. And this time I promise you I'll cut his trail and run him down."

"If I tell you where he is," said Joey, "will you go there and have your talk with him and come straight home, back to us?"

"Why, yes, boy, I will," said Rush mildly, and when Amy, amazed and irritated, started to speak, he said, "Shush." To Joey, he said, "Where is he?"

Joey said, "When, just now, you named your journey you left out the most important place, Niles Station. He's with the Jowetts. They out-smarted you."

Rush considered this. He realized the idea was startling but possible.

"To folks like them kin is the most important thing in the world," said Joey. "I thought the story they told you was mighty skinny-thin. All it said, when you come right down to it, was that they wanted you out of their country and quick." The boy opened his arithmetic book, took out a blank sheet of paper, laid the paper and a pencil

130

before Rush, and said, "Draw. Draw as well as you can recall the cabins and buildings around it."

Rush wet the pencil tip on his lip, pondered, and drew a sketchy diagram.

He said, "This long thing is the cabin. This little square just to the side of it is the privy. This little square to the other side is the smokehouse."

Joey looked at it, musing. "He was somewhere close, we can be sure of that. He'd hide where he could see and hear as much as he could. It wouldn't be the privy because he couldn't be certain you might not want to use it while you were there. Was there a padlock on the smokehouse?"

"I don't recall," said Rush, absorbed despite himself.

"All smokehouses have padlocks, they have to have. Was this one locked or unlocked?"

"I didn't notice. I had other things to think about."

"He was in the smokehouse," said Joey definitely. "While you were gossipin' and such with Mayhew and Wilcox and Palmer, he was in the smokehouse, peepin' out at you and eavesdroppin'."

"Do you think so, Amy?" asked Rush.

"How would I know?" said Amy, a little unstrung herself.

"They hustled him into it just before you came up," said Joey, riding it as hard as he could.

"When do you set out again?" asked Amy.

"I'm not sure," said Rush. "In a day or two, probably. That'll give him time to think it's all over."

"And are you going to visit Mr. Wilcox Jowett again?" said Joey, pressing him. "And maybe take a careless look into the smokehouse this time?"

"How do I know?" said Rush angrily. "If it will make you any happier, yes."

"And if he isn't there?" said Amy.

"I'll visit the young clerk in the Thomas L. Grayville office. And grind it out of *him*."

"And if he's not there?" said Amy.

"I'll talk to the bartender at the Checker Front. That thing with Holburn was set up with his consent and aid. He'll know about Hankinson." Rush paused. "And he'll remember Holburn."

"But if he really doesn't know?"

"Then I'll go on to Hayes at Lister, and if I have to, on to whatever I can pick up at Spencer Eakins's place. It's not impossible, actually, that Hankinson is *there,* in person."

"It seems pretty hopeless," said Amy.

"A man like Hankinson leaves tracks," said Rush. "He can't help it. It'll just take time."

"If I never see you again," said Amy, almost inaudibly, "what shall I name the baby?"

"Rann," said Rush.

"I'm not a baby anymore, and haven't been for years," said Joey, wandering, dazed, lost in the mist of their words. "Besides, I've already got a name."

XI

NEXT MORNING, Amy had Rush's favorite breakfast for him, buckwheat cakes, the batter of which she had put to rise the night before in a crock, and which cooked up as light and high and non-doughy as sponge cake; hog jowl sliced a little less than a half inch thick and oven baked, not fried, to a honey-colored yellowness that crumbled and powdered on the tongue like super-bacon; and scrambled eggs pioneer style, the whites streaking the yolks. He ate his cakes with a pat of butter, but no syrup. If he took it into his appetite for something sweet he ate a little jam, and always with a spoon, like a dessert.

"That's better than half-cooked campfire corn dodgers, isn't it?" said Amy.

"Don't run down corn dodgers," said Rush severely.

When they'd finished, Rush said, "Joey, did your father have some kind of hiding place around the house?"

"Two, of course," said Joey.

"What do you mean, of course?" said Rush.

"One that was the big secret," said Joey. "For valuable things, that I should know about, he said, if anything should happen to him. It was on the shelf of the fireplace in the empty bedroom.

I looked at it before I left. Nothing there. I'd looked other times. I never seen nothing at all there but once a busted swallow's egg. I always figgered he never had no real call to use it."

"What about the other place?" asked Rush.

"That one was his, private. I wasn't even supposed to know about it."

"Did you look in that one before you left?"

"I just said it was his, private."

"Answer my question."

"What kind of a hound dog do you think I am?"

"Did you?"

"Yes, sir."

"That's better," said Rush. "What did you find?"

"Nothing, Rush. And that's the funny thing. By the purest accident a few days before I happened to peep around the door jamb and see him put something into it. He must have took it out again next day. Though I didn't see him do it and him and me just nacherly knowed what each other was doing when we was indoors. You know how it gets to be when two people live together."

"You mean curious and sneaky," said Amy. "Yes, I know."

"With women it's being curious and sneaky," explained Rush. "With men it's being protective." After a minute, he added, "Where is this second place?"

"Of all things, it's in the empty bedroom, too. The room that used to be grandma's. But it's not in the fireplace, or around it. It's under a loose board of the floor that fits into the southwest corner. There's a tin box there. He never keeps it locked but when I looked just before I left it had the same old papers in it, no new ones."

"What are these papers?" asked Rush.

"Many's the rainy afternoon I studied them when pa was away someplace like to Pelburg," said Joey. "Let's see. His marriage license to ma. The deed to the house and the land around it, chains and links and so on. The Department of Indian Affairs papers for his cattle on the Bannock Reservation. Papers like that. They must be still there if you want to look them over."

"I do," said Rush. "You're sure there's nothing new?"

"Take my oath on it."

"I'm not sure a child of his years should be using the word oath," said Amy.

"There's no harm in the word oath itself," said Rush. "The kind you mean is something different. Say a few of the other kind for her, Joey—the kind a teamster uses to a balking horse."

"Let's change the subject," said Amy icily.

Perhaps fifty yards behind Rush's cottage was a sizable gulch that acted as rear property line for half a dozen ranges and homesteads. It was the route, Rush was sure, that Rann Clark's killers had used.

Rush's cottage, abutting it, was only a short distance from Rann Clark's, which also abutted it. This morning, Rush, afoot, took it. He had taken it many times. Joey had taken it when he had dashed over with the news of his father's murder.

When he came to a place where the left-hand wall, undercut, had eventually fallen and a steep opening rose to the upper level, he knew this was the Clark boundary and turned and climbed. He came out, as he had done so many times before, into a knee-high thicket of jackpines.

He paused and looked around. Beyond the edge of the jackpines was a narrow stretch of grass, the old and dead intermingled with this year's, and a picket fence, a side view of Rann Clark's kitchen garden; behind the fence and garden was the back porch of the big white house. He crossed. He had his hands on the fence, about to vault it, when, glancing down, he saw the blood in the grass by his boot toe.

He bent over and examined it.

Set in the ground was a cold frame, where Rann raised seedling plants for transplanting. It was a squarish frame of four planks, covered with two window sashes and their panes. Because of the season, because it was in disuse at the moment, one of the windows, the front one, had been stacked on the other, the rear one. This formed a sort of little cave under the rear sash. The blood

137

on the grass outside led to the planking, inside, and back into this little cave.

Curious, Rush lifted aside the windows. He understood the blood instantly. Some kind of small animal had littered back in there, picking a hidden spot with true maternal instinct.

Now, as a test in his old skill in reading sign, Rush inspected things carefully and tried to decide what kind of animal, precisely, had littered in Rann Clark's cold frame.

First, from, the tracks, a dog. Just a dog. Then, putting his heart into it, Rush saw very small gray hairs, inside-of-the-ear hairs; long silky white hairs, belly hairs; and stiff black hairs, back hairs. A black dog with a white belly. There was something else, too, in the frame: a saucer, grimy now, which had been used for milk for the puppies and beef bones for the mother. Rann had been feeding them.

He had been feeding them out of the compassion of his soul, for they were strays. Rann Clark owned no dogs.

Rush climbed the fence, angled across the garden, and mounted to the back porch.

All movement of air stopped. A gloom and coolness came over everything. He looked at the sky. There was a covering of sooty clouds, knotted, bulging, veined with lampblack. There was going to be a rain—a big one and quick, a cloudburst.

He tried the knob of the back door. It was locked, as he had expected, from the sheriff's official locking at the time of Rann's removal. But Rush's special key was in its place above the lintel; he used it and entered. The kitchen had been well scrubbed and gave off the faint scent of home-leached lye. Everything was in order, as it had been left by Amy and her friends in the death-cleaning. He passed the stove, left brighter by those feminine fingers than Rann had seen it for many a year, went out of the kitchen, ascended the stairs, and came into the upper hall. He knew the house well from the past, and which room had always been referred to as grandma's room. Here he stepped inside.

It was a low room running across the rear of the house, its window looking out onto the tin roof of the projecting kitchen below. The wallpaper was of purple-pink morning glories climbing a dusty gold trellis. There was a steel engraving on the wall of a little girl, up to the top of her button shoes in snow, peering longingly, hands cupped to cheeks, into the show window of a saloon— not at a display of fancy cordials as it seemed at first glance, but at a boozy but happy daddy sprawled at a table beyond.

The room was empty of furniture and the broad floorboards were bare.

Rush went immediately to the southwest corner.

The corner plank came up easily and there, beneath it, lay the tin box. Rush took it up and examined its contents. They were exactly as Joey had described them, nothing more, nothing less, nothing of interest.

After a moment of thought, Rush reached back into the hole between the joists and found it— the folded paper. Placed there by Rann beyond Joey's reach.

Now, outside, clouds seemed to split in fiery violet cracks, and the water came—not in drops or needles, but in great gushes. Thunder coughed and exploded, the tin roof outside the window roared and rattled and groaned, and lightning crackled like splitting trees. When you not only saw lightning but heard it, you knew it was over you like a tent.

The room darkened. Rush unfolded the paper and read it with difficulty. It said:

This was a little experience I had some time back and can't get out of my mind. I figure I had better put it on paper before I get it all mixed up in my memory, if I have not already got it mixed up. The sun had gone down maybe half an hour before and I was moving west through grassy swales and rises when I saw this herd of cattle appear from nowhere it seemed, in little clots and bunches, until at last they came to something like eight or nine hundred head. There was nothing on the plain and then there was them. They were being driven by riders at point and drag and all and there were no two ways about it, it was a trail herd, just getting onto the move, just a dusk-dark. The drovers didn't pay no attention to me and I didn't make out to pay no attention to them. Then I passed this bowl of grass and could see where they had been hid and bedded. Bedded during daylight, it seemed. I kept on and reached my destination, the ranch building, about an hour and a half later. The man was before the ranch house leaning against the well smoking a corncob pipe. I got my business with him over and he was thankful and overjoyed and then I told him what I'd seen because it was on his land. He did not pay any heed to it but said they was going into a bedground and a heap of trail herders used other folks' land these days on the move but those cattle were not going into a bedground, they were coming out, because they had all the signs of it. Joey, if your prying fingers ever find this and your poor spelling ever makes any sense out of it forget it because sometime, maybe years from now, knowledge of it could mean your death. Mind what I say, Joey. You hear!

Rush replaced the paper as he had found it.

So Rann Clark had at one time been on Spencer Eakins's land.

And later, maybe years later, who could say, it had killed him, hadn't it? Rush replaced the floor plank and stood up.

A voice from behind him said, "Howdy, Rush. They told me I'd find you here."

Rush turned.

Tate, I-Buy-and-Sell-Everything, the old man who had been one of Rush's closest friends, walked into the room. His pinched little face was like a crimson nut coated with water and drops of water fell from his beak of a nose to his bony protruding chin. He was a mass of yellow oilskins, much too large for his spindly body, and they left a watery trail behind him as he advanced. Rush said, "How did you know it was going to rain when you left Pelburg?"

"I didn't," said Tate. "These are yours. Mrs. Ledderman loaned them to me when I stopped at your house for you."

"You ride all the way out from Pelburg just to see me?" said Rush.

"Correct."

"Well, here I am," said Rush. "What's on your mind?"

"I've got a cousin in Jennington. He likes to be helpful to me when and if such an occasion comes up. I wired him to keep a eye on the so-called Grayville office there. The place that's Hankinson's headquarters. He just sent me a telegram saying the door's locked and there's a card in the window saying *Closed Temporarily on Account of Repairs.* The shades're pulled. Even that young man you told me about has gone off. *Repairs* is right."

Startled, Rush said, "What do you make of it?"

"That you've really scared him," said Tate. "Not personally—don't imagine he scares very easy personally being in the business he is—but scared him about his set-up. Here you come up out of nowhere and cause him big trouble at places of his that you're not even supposed to ever of heard about. Things are pretty serious from his point of view. You could mighty well blow up his whole blamed operation for him."

"Maybe I have already," said Rush.

"Not by a long shot. It was flourishing too mightily, showing too much profit. All they'll do is adjust. And then later, when things have quieted down, they'll open up shop again, maybe bigger'n better than before."

"Adjust?"

"They've made out to close the Jennington

143

office, ain't they? Ten to one, the Checker Front Saloon has became the Mecca or something, under new management, Hayes's place at Lister has a different barman, and the Spencer Eakins spread has a shuffle of new faces, shuttled in from somewhere else, that don't know nothing about nothing. And there goes your backtrack, son."

When Rush didn't answer, Tate said, "Until."

"Until what?"

"Until they see what damage you've already did them, if any."

"I don't think they can work it," said Rush thoughtfully.

"Of course they can work it. I won't say that's the way they'll do it, but they'll do something. They know it's going to be all over soon anyways."

"Then they know something I don't know," said Rush. "I'm just starting."

"I asked you the other night if we was friends again," said Tate. "And you slid around it. I'll try 'er once more. Are we?"

"Yes, Harlowe," said Rush. "I wasn't myself the other night."

"That's better," said Tate. "Hankinson is the hub to this whole wheel. I got ways of knowing this for a fact. If you want me to, I'll tell you what I'll do. I'll get word to him that I have your word o' honor that, as of now, you'll leave him be if he'll leave you be."

Rush was petrified with anger. After a second, he said, "Wild horses couldn't drag such a promise from me! And what kind of man are you? How could you get word to him?"

"In a long and tedious way I don't care to discuss. It's a heap too dangerous for me to even think about."

Rush said, "For old times' sake, I'll just put it this way: *Goodbye*."

"Listen, Rush," said Tate soberly. "You can't win. It's beyond you. The first thing Hankinson will do is find out just who you are and how to locate you—and that won't be hard, not for a man like Hankinson. Then you could be all the champion gunfighters in the world rolled into one and your life would go whenever he flicked the ash off his cigar, gunfire at your back out of a alleymouth, ambush from a gully, a derringer from a loafer in a doorway."

"I've faced all that before."

"Then you can thank God you've survived, for it's a meat grinder when the man with the bankroll says do it. Are Mrs. Ledderman and Joey as good at it as you?"

"What do you mean?" asked Rush.

"Who knows what will happen in a thing like this?"

"No," said Rush quietly. "I won't deal with a skunk."

Tate said, "And neither will I. And by that I

mean a man who would trade off his wife and a little boy to satisfy a grudge, a man like you've just showed me."

He took off the oilskins and dropped them in a heap on the floor. "You tell me goodbye. All right, I tell you goodbye. Here's your slicker. I want to be shed of anything that belongs to you." He turned and walked from the room. Outside, thunder crashed and water hammered the window pane.

Rush stood alone in the room as the storm clamored.

He knew that he had done right.

He knew that no word of honor, nor promise, nor anything of the sort would ever hold as a working bond with Hankinson. If it was necessary or convenient for him that Amy or Joey die, then they would die. And no agreement would prevent it. A man like Hankinson did not function through words.

His next step would come soon, and it wouldn't be a lot of foolishness about changing things at the Checker Front, or Hayes's saloon, or the Spencer Eakins place.

It would be dredging up a half dozen more Holburns, deadlier and meaner this time to make sure, and turning them loose on him—giving them free choice of manner and style.

Tate had been right about that part of it. This was what he was up against now, the ambush, the hidden doorway, the volley in the back.

The rain had stopped, the clouds had gone over and past, but the gulch, Rush realized, would be a fury of froth and turbulence, so he returned home by the path, the slightly longer route. The after-rain sun was like a bucket of fire.

Amy came to the gate to meet him and Joey was behind her, leading his bay mare, saddled and ready to go. He sensed their urgency.

"What's up?" be asked.

Amy said, "John Sutton just sent a man in. His horse was lathered from hard riding. You're wanted in a hurry. At the place where Tamarack Branch runs under Culvert 147. They had last night what we had just now. There was a flash flood in the branch that washed out about six miles and more of our new road and Mr. Sutton wants you up there to look it over and give him your ideas on what you want him to do."

Culvert 147 was about twelve miles away, if you took it cross-country, diagonally.

As he sprang into the saddle, Rush said, "I don't know when I'll be back. Not before suppertime, I'd say. It could be not too bad or it could cost us a lot of money."

He didn't walk his mare, but he didn't over-ride her, didn't push her, despite the lathered horse Amy had spoken of, for she'd had enough punishment recently and besides, there was really not too much rush; any wickedness that had happened at 147 was over and done with, and speed wouldn't actually help things.

His line of travel was east by a little north, beginning as a slice through the Rann Clark land, then passing through brushy young timber, spruce and arrow-thin cottonwood hazy around their bases with sumac and scrub masses. The timber—but not the brush—stopped, the grade of the earth began to slope, and he knew he was crossing the place he had several times heard called Settlers Sink. In his travels, he had heard the term *sink* used, and misused a good many different ways locally, for everything from a neighborhood puddle of quicksand to the Colorado desert. A true sink, a prospector had once told him, was a place that had some kind of water or stream with no on-the-surface outlet; it didn't flow off, it just went into the ground some place.

The hollow proved to be of considerable size and its center, Rush saw when he came to it, was turfy and had been cleared of brush with ax strokes. Halfway up the far slope a group of springs merged into a sluggish stream. The stream flowed down into the floor of the hollow, made a small loop, and disappeared into a crack of limestone which lay exposed in the thin topsoil. Rush climbed his mount up out of the depression, and was immediately in the grassland.

He set his mare again on her course, east by a little north.

About an hour and a half later, he came up to the cabin he had by now expected in his natural line of travel, Guffy's. He came up to it from the back.

In that hour and a half, he had become convinced he had made a mistake in interpreting Rann Clark's paper. The paper under the floor had not referred to the basin at the Spencer Eakins place up near Lister; it had referred to a hollow right here in the locality, here at home. It had referred to Settlers Sink.

He slid from his saddle, ground-reined his mare, and circled the cabin on foot.

Two men were sitting in the shade of the cabin dog run, chatting amiably.

Guffy and Hankinson.

XII

GUFFY, BLUBBERY, stubble-faced, dirty-clothed, was seated on a low three-legged stool, a cauldron of steaming hot water between his legs, plucking birds. The birds were meadow larks. By one of his ankles was a pile of the dead unplucked songsters, small and chunky and brown, with their yellow breasts and black neckties, very sad looking. By Guffy's other ankle were the plucked birds waiting to be gutted and dressed, pitiful white wax lumps. He would pick up a bird by its claws, dip it in the water, pull off its head, nip off its lower legs with tinsnips, pluck it, and drop it nude with the other wax lumps. Beside him, in tan twill and calf-high walking boots, sat Hankinson, his furrowed cheeks relaxed, even smiling. Across Hankinson's lap was a gun.

It was a gun of a type that Rush had seen many times elsewhere, an old muzzle loader, big-bored and octagonal-barreled, converted to percussion cap. Rush knew it was loaded and ready to go— not only because it showed a new cap on its lock, but because he knew Hankinson was the kind of man who would fire a muzzle loader properly. When you fire one, the next thing you do, immediately, is reload it, even before you investigate your quarry. Fire, and reload. A man with an unloaded rifle in his hand might as well be holding a stick of kindling wood.

Rush glanced quickly at the birds and speculated on the size of the shot. It would be small, of course, but even bird-shot could rip you like a gang-saw.

"Like I told you," Hankinson was saying, "I don't sleep well at night, and have these little fevers."

"That's all over and did with now," said Guffy. "You're okay now. When the fevers took hold of my daddy they never gave him nothing but meadow lark broth."

Rush had heard this so-called family remedy many and many a time.

He knew that his best range, of course, was nothing at all. When he came into their view and stopped he judged them to be about thirteen feet away. He carried his right hand as his masters had long ago taught him, and experience had confirmed. Carelessly limp, just below his thigh-bone.

The problem here was an interesting one. It was not Guffy. Guffy would get his due, in good time. It was a problem mainly in mechanics: how mechanically quick was Hankinson's reflexes, and how mechanically smooth was the action of the old muzzle loader.

It was practically pointing at him now. If

Hankinson was a quick thinker and a quick mover, Rush would scarcely stand a chance.

"I guess we'll have to wait and see," said Rush sardonically, thinking aloud. They flicked their eyes upward, and stared at him.

"Well, there he is," said Guffy quietly. "Does he know you by sight?"

"By sight," said Hankinson. He was careful not to move his hand, the hand that was so close to the gun butt.

He missed that chance, thought Rush. *What about the next? And maybe that cocking-thumb can move like a snake's tongue.*

To Hankinson, Rush said, "Those three men, that scum you paid a thousand dollars to kill Rann Clark, I killed them without warning, gave them no more chance than they gave him. I was saving a little of the same for you. But the Good Lord has given you a break. He has put a shotgun in your hands. Fire it!"

"Why would I have this Rann Clark killed?" argued Hankinson. His eyes remained steady, but his scarred cheeks quivered slightly, showing his tension, and the little bead of moisture gathered at the corner of his lip. "I never even saw this Clark."

"Why would you have him killed, that's what I wondered," said Rush. "Until it drove me half crazy. But now I know."

"Then tell me."

"The days of the real cattle droves," said Rush, "the big ones, the long ones, from back-country hundreds and hundreds of miles to the nearest railhead, are over. The country now is getting crisscrossed with track, and a rancher takes his cattle to the closest chutes—chutes never too far away, when you think of the old days. The long droves are gone but the cattle are thicker than ever, and the rustlers more than ever, and the rustling easier than ever. In the old days, a big herd on the long-move was raided by Indians and renegades and rustler bands, and losses could be great from a single raid."

His listeners watched him, taut.

Rush continued. "So the days of the noisy marauding, with whoops and hollers and gunshots and sometimes war paint and eagle feathers are gone."

They stayed motionless.

"The new rustling is different," said Rush. "It's pulled off quiet and sly. *In small lots.* In small lots, but the sum total of cows stolen, I'm told, is so enormous you'd hardly believe it."

"There are cows taken, all right," said Guffy. "I'm a rancher and I ought to know. But not near as many as you're making out. A few. Butcher cattle, mostly. A little fresh beef for the nearest village meatshop."

"Some go that way, of course," said Rush. "But only a very small percentage. Mainly, they find their way to loading chutes and end up in some eastern slaughter house."

Still the tableau in the dog run sat frozen.

"This stuff is usually handled in small bunches," said Rush. "In bunches of six or eight or ten. Not many, Mr. Hankinson, do it like you do."

"Like I do?" said Hankinson. "What are you talking about?"

"I'm talking about gathering these stolen cows, these small bunches, together at special collecting points, like the Spencer Eakins place, for instance, and then droving them to some crooked shipping yards, maybe at a big railroad town like Jennington. I'll bet you, yourself, personally own yards and chutes at Jennington."

"These are pretty wild guesses," said Hankinson.

"Such ownership can be proved," said Rush.

"As a matter of fact, as you must certainly already know, I own both pens and yards and chutes in Jennington," said Hankinson. "I need them in my business and they're a matter of public knowledge, so what of it?"

Rush said, "I've no idea how many of these collecting points you've established. But the Spencer Eakins place is one, and Guffy's here is another."

"Leave me out of this," said Guffy. He tried to look righteously indignant.

"I'm talking about Settlers Sink," said Rush.

154

"Rann Clark saw it in use. He mentioned it to you, you told Hankinson and Hankinson sent three lice down from Lister to shut his mouth."

He watched Hankinson's gunhand. It didn't move.

Hankinson said calmly, "I got news for you."

"I don't need it," said Rush.

"It didn't happen the way you say at all," said Hankinson. "Settlers Sink is a cattle cache, that I admit. But Guffy's, not mine. I've bought stolen cattle from him—that too I admit—but I had nothing to do with the killing of your friend. It was Guffy himself who did it, entirely without my knowledge. He went up to Clark's house and gunned him down at the breakfast table, without a word, as he sat there helpless."

"Don't do it!" pleaded Guffy. "Don't do it, Mr. Hankinson, don't sit there and lie me into my coffin!"

And that was it, that was the diversion Hankinson had wanted. His fingers flew to the breech of the old shotgun and Rush shot him five times. He shot him as he had never shot a man before. The enclosure of the dog run pounded and hammered with the gunshots, but it was as though he were stone deaf; his ears simply didn't register them. Nor was he aware of the pistol in his hand. It was as though Rush were in a trance, watching Hankinson tumble to the floor among the meadow larks, his eyeballs upturned like hard-boiled eggs, the twill across his heart jerking crazily, rhythmically beneath the heavy slugs.

His rage came and went and a dullness came over him. He couldn't bring himself to turn on Guffy. He couldn't bring himself to shoot a gibbering imbecile, and Guffy was infantile from terror.

Rush said, "Saddle up. We're going into Pelburg, to the sheriff."

He took the man's plump hand and helped him from the dog run to the yard. Guffy moved almost as though he were blind.

XIII

TEN DAYS LATER, just after sundown, in the cool of the evening, the three of them, Amy, Rush, and Joey, sat in straight-backed kitchen chairs along the outside wall of the cottage, talking it all over, watching the stars swing up into the indigo sky, enjoying the soft touch of the prairie breeze. Rush said, "Guffy has talked so much that even the sheriff and the U. S. marshal are almost tired of listening to him. The set-up is busted, of course. If Guffy himself doesn't hang, he'll sure wish he had by the time the prison doors swing open to let him out. I know, because I've eaten off that iron table, as the boys say."

"It started here and it ended here," said Amy.

"It was here all the time," corrected Rush. "Guffy's was one of Hankinson's stations. Joey, Guffy has give you the bitch and her offspring. One of his hands will be bringing them in to you any time now. Tell us about 'em again."

"Mr. Guffy had this black and white hunting dog," said Joey. "She was going to have puppies and got nervous—"

"Piccalilli on chocolate cake," said Rush.

"She got nervous and wandered away to have them some place safe," said Joey. "She wandered up the gulch, and up behind our garden, and had

157

them back in our cold frame. I found them, and told my father, and he fed them until they were big enough to handle. Then he took them back."

"Took them back," said Rush. "Down the gulch. Past Settlers Sink. At the wrong time. He mentioned the strange goings-on to Guffy and sealed his doom."

"I got to love those puppies," said Joey. "You won't believe it, but there was one who kept trying to shake hands, all by himself, without my teaching him, and with all four feet at the same time!"

Amy looked meaningly at Rush.

Rush nodded in answer. *You'd think he'd hate their memory,* he was thinking.

A buckboard rolled up and John Sutton climbed out.

The extra chair, the company chair, was waiting. He lowered himself into it.

It was three or four minutes before anyone spoke. Then Sutton said, "Road fixed after washout. Better'n before."

"Fine," said Rush.

"Stolen horse back where it belongs," said Sutton. "Jest come wanderin' in."

"Fine," said Rush.

"How's Mrs. Sutton's tooth?" asked Amy.

"See for yourself," said Sutton. He produced a small something that looked like a chunk of bone in the moonglow.

"Pulled it yourself?" said Amy, when she could get her breath. "With pinchers?"

"Jumped it for her," said Sutton.

To jump a tooth, an ancient practice of the eastern mountains, from which much of the local population derived, you took a nail—a horseshoe nail was best because it had the most substantial head—placed the head against the bad tooth at the edge of the gum, and hit the other end, the point of the nail, smartly and powerfully with a hammer. No anesthetic, of course. The pain was excruciating.

"Did she scream?" asked Amy.

"No, ma'am. She grinned."

"Grinned!"

"Fact is, she wants to try it again. With a couple others."

Rush risked a comment. "You give her a little sup of whisky first?" Mrs. Sutton was a notorious teetotaler.

"Not a sup," said Sutton. "I followed the old directions."

"What are the old directions?" asked Amy.

Sutton said, "Get that tooth drunk, not halfway but *drunk*."

Center Point Large Print
600 Brooks Road / PO Box 1
Thorndike, ME 04986-0001 USA

(207) 568-3717

US & Canada:
1 800 929-9108
www.centerpointlargeprint.com